Gerald Massey

Havelock's March

And other Poems

Gerald Massey

Havelock's March
And other Poems

ISBN/EAN: 9783337206369

Printed in Europe, USA, Canada, Australia, Japan

Cover: Foto ©Andreas Hilbeck / pixelio.de

More available books at **www.hansebooks.com**

HAVELŌCK'S MARCH

AND OTHER POEMS.

BY

GERALD MASSEY.

LONDON:

TRÜBNER & CO., PATERNOSTER ROW.

1861.

THE Author has re-cast and reprinted his BURNS Brochure in this volume. He has also included some half-dozen pieces from "All the Year Round," and would here record his most cordial acknowledgments of the kindness and liberality of Mr. Charles Dickens.

CONTENTS.

CHRISTIE'S POEMS.

DOWN IN THE VILLAGE.

PROEM

DEDICATORY TO

LADY MARIAN ALFORD.

LADY MARIAN.

In her Ancestral tree's old smiling shade,
Spencer and Milton sang, and Shakespeare played.
I cannot prophesy immortal fame,
And endless honour for my lady's name
Thro' my poor Verse; but it shall surely give
All that it has, and long as it may live.

She heard my children singing in the street,
And smiled down on them starry-clear and sweet,
But halfway up in Heaven, and far from me,
As Shakespeare's Juliet in her balcony;
A golden Creature, all too rare to stay,
With waving white hand she would pass away!

Now I have seen her; heard her voice To-day,
And toucht her hand; enricht my life for aye:
The thought in sunbeams radiantly upsprings,
To smile out in the saddest face of things.
After the gloom is gone, the worst is passed,
I know you, my good Fairy, found at last.

Tho' poor, and grim to tears, our life might be,
We had proud visions in our poverty !
My Princess too, with darkly sparkling e'en,
As I lay dreaming, over me would lean ;
And now the silken clue of hidden power,
Hath led me to her beauty in its bower.

Lady ! Giorgione should have painted you
With live warm flesh-tints golden thro' and thro' ;
The sun-soul making luminous its prison   .
With sunken splendours, rarer than have risen ;
Bird-peeps of brightness—dawn-dew—smiling fire
Full of all freshness as a spring-wood quire ;

A glow and glory of impetuous blood ;
Brave spirits that crowd all sail to take the flood
Of large, abounding life, that in the sun
Heaves flashing, with a frolic fringe of fun ;
A happy wit ! creative genius proved
In Pictures that Angelico would have loved :

A stately soul : yet with a laugh that brings
Echoes from Girlhood's heaven as it rings !
And that fine spirit of motion's airy charm,
Which hovers glancing round the flower of form :
A lofty lady of a proud old race,
Recklessly splendid in her gifts and grace.

Yet, as the life of some tall, towery tree
Climbs till atop it laughs exultingly
With all its leaves, using its pride of place
To look both earth and heaven full in the face!
Thus—up thro' bole and branch of wealth and blood,
Breaks out her noble natural Womanhood.

No fear of England's great old Houses when
Such glorious women give us noble men,
And sway the heart o' the people sovereignly
As the Moon sways the heavings of the sea,
To touch its darkness with her lovelier light,
And mould to loftier shape its climbing might.

Their foes may rave, but, far off is their fall,
Whose glory is the heritage of all!
Who grew some grain we long shall save for seed;
Who man the gap for England in her need.
All who love England think with holy pride
Of all who for her like De Norman died.

My Lady Marian, you are good, and true;
Most bountiful, and gracious as the dew:
And glad Hearts—wing'd with Blessings—follow you
Far as the Earth is green, or Heaven is blue;
But, dear my lady, there is work to do
In England yet, and royal work for you.

Why leave your own free air, and English Home,
For Paris—that Slave-Dancer—or for Rome?
With all their lustres, dazzlingly displayed,
They cannot match the sweetness of our shade;
Our leafier pathways cool with gladder green;
Our Hearts, whose heavings lift you up—our Queen.

Much Mother's Milk wants sweetening with the Balms
That you can bring; much need of more than Alms!
In eyes wide open souls lie fast asleep;
With daylight on the face hearts darkly weep;
Our world has many a ward where wounds and wails
Cry for a thousand Florence Nightingales.

I know that Knowledge thro' our Shire doth trail
With slow illumination of a snail!
But still we dream of some bright better day,
And while we sleep the great Dawn comes our way.
Think How long God's love brooded over Earth
Before she quickened for her noblest Birth!

Oh, they shall bless you down in pit and den,—
Transforming slowly into Women and Men;
And smile, as leaves out-smile in first spring-hours,
With livelier green, while fall the singing showers;
Or as the winter mosses round your trees
Look up and smile at their good influences.

Your pardon, Lady, if my unskilled word,
Like a bad player, should mistake the chord!
No churlish charge, no plea of parasite,
Is mine; but leal heart-service of a knight
Who in old days had fought for you and bled;
Going to death as 'twere a bridal bed.

Our lost " Maid Marian " bore your name, and she
Yet works a very tender ministry;
And, somehow, when of her we sit and think
Our hearts touch you by an invisible link.
Sacred to her, my sadder verses take;
And kindly think of them for Marian's sake.

Room for my Sea-Kings too, your heart will make,
From young Sir William Peel, to old King Hako.
You have the spirit born of the salt spray
That snuffs the sea-breeze meadowy miles away;
The Norse blood running seaward round the world,
That leaves the Saxon inland closely curled.

You love our Heroes! and you might have been
In battle-need our Boadicea Queen!
And stood up to the full majestic height
In your war-chariot beckoning on the fight:
A famous victory you would have wrought,
Or with your heroes fallen as you fought.

NATIONAL.

HAVELOCK'S MARCH.

The Revolt.

Come hither my brave Soldier boy, and sit you by my
      side,
To hear a tale, a fearful tale, a glorious tale of pride;
How Havelock with his handful, all so faithful, and
      so few,
Held on in that far Indian land, to bear our England
      through   [wrath;
Her pass of bloodiest peril, and her reddest sea of
· And strode like Paladins of old on their avenging path.
Tho' clothes were drencht, and flesh was parcht, and
      bones were chilled with cold,
The gallant hearts never gave up; they never loosed
      their hold;
But fought right on, and triumphed! O but eyes
      rained as we read
How proudly every place was filled, with living and
      with dead.

The dark death-circle narrowed round our little
    English band :
The stillness of a brooding storm lay on the east-
    ern land ;
The false Sepoy stoopt lower for his spring, and, in
    his eye
A bloody light was burning on them, as he glided by :
Old Horrors rose, and leered at them, from out the
    tide of time,—
The peering peaks of War's old world, whose brows
    were stained with crime !
The conscious Silence was but dumb, a cursed plot to
    hide ;
The darkness only a mask of Death, ready to slip aside.
Under the leafy palms they lay, and through their
    gay green crown,
Our English saw no Storm roll up : no Fate swift
    flaming down.

At last it came.   The Rebel drum was heard at dead
    of night :
They dasht in dust the only torch that showed the
    face of Right !
Again the Devil clutches at his lost throne of the
    earth,
And sends a people, smit with plague of madness,
    howling forth.

As in a Demon's dream they swarm from horrible
  hiding nooks ;
Red Murder stabs the air, and lights their way with
  bloody looks!
Snuffing the smell of human blood, the cruel Moloch
  stands ;
Hearing the cry of "Kill! Kill! Kill!" and claps
  his gory hands.
At dead of night, while England slept, the fearful
  vision came,
She lookt, and with a dawn of hell the East was all
  a-flame.

Stern tidings came to Havelock, of legions in revolt :
" The traitors turn upon us, and the eaters of our
  salt,
Subtle as death, and false as hell, and cruel as the
  grave,
Have sworn to rend us by the root; be quick, if ye
  would save ;
The wild beasts bloody and obscene, mad-drunk with
  gore and lust,
Have wreaked a horrible vengeance on our England
  rolled in dust."
And such a withering wind doth blow, such fearful
  sounds it brings,
The soul with shudders tries to shake off creeping
  thoughts and things !

A vast invisible Terror twines its fingers in the hair,
With one hand feeling for the throat; a hand that
    will not spare.

They slew the grizzled Warrior, who to them had
    been so true;
The ruddy stripling with frank eyes of bonny
    English blue;
They slew the Maiden as she slept; the Mother great
    with child;
The Babe, that smiled up in their face, they stabbed
    it as it smiled.
The piteous, pleading, hoary hair, they draggled in
    red mire;
And mocked the dying as they dasht out, frantic
    from the fire,
To fall upon their Tulwars, hacked to death; the bayonet
Held up some child; the devils danced around it
    writhing yet:
Warm flesh, that kindled so with life, was torn, and
    slowly hewn,
To daintiest morsels for the feast where death began
    too soon.

Our English girls, whose sweet red blood went dan-
    cing on its way,
A merry marriage-maker quick for its near wedding-
    day,—

All life awaiting for the breath of Love's sweet south
    to blow,
And budding bridal roses ripe with secret balms
    should flow—
They stripped them naked as they were born; naked
    along the street,
In their own blood they made them dip their delicate
    white feet!
With some last rag of shelter the poor helpless dar-
    ling tries
To hide her from the cruel hell of those devouring
    eyes;
Then, plucking at the skirts of Death, she prayer-
    fully doth cling,
To hide her from the eyes that still gloat round her in
    a ring.

The Avengers.

" Now, Soldiers of our England, let your love arise in
    power ;   [hour :
For never yet was greater need than in this awful
Together stand like old true-hearts that never fear nor
    flinch ;
With feet that have been shod for death, never to
    yield an inch.
Our Empire is a Ship on fire, before a howling wind,
With such a smoke of torment, as 'twould make high
    heaven blind !   -
Wild Ruin waves his flag of flame, and ye must spring
    on deck,
And quench the fire in blood, and save our treasures
    from the wreck."
Many a time has England thought she sent her
    bravest forth ;   [worth.
But never went more gallant men, of more heroic

Hungry and lean, thro' rain and mire, our war-wolves
    grimly go,
On their long march, that shall not mete the red
    grave of the foe :

Like winter trees stripped to their naked strength of
    heart and arm,
That glory in their grimness as they tussle with the
    storm!
Only a handful few and stern, and few and stern their
    words;
Fierce meaning in their eyes that meet and strike out
    sparks like swords!
And there goes Havelock! leading the Forlorn Hope
    of our land;
The quick heart spurring at their side; the banner of
    their band:
Kindled, but calm, along their ranks his steady eye
    doth run,   [his gun.
As marksman seeks the death-line down the level of

Beneath the whitening snows of age his spirit ardours
    glow,
As glow the fragrant fires of spring in flowers beneath
    the snow.
Look in his grave and martial face, with God's dear
    pity toucht;
A saviour soul doth sanctify the sword his hand hath
    clutcht: [pray,
A little while his silent thoughts have gone within to
And send a farewell of the heart to the dear ones far
    away.

He prays to God to light him thro' the perilous
    darkness, when
He grapples with the beasts of blood, and quells them
    in their den.
And now his look is lifted in the light of some far
    goal ;
His lips the living trumpet of a grey-haired seer's soul.

On the housetops of Allahabad black, scowling brows
    were bent,
In hate, and deep, still curses, on our heroes as they
    went
To fight their hundred-days-long fight; all true as
    their good steel,
The Highlanders of Havelock, the Fusileers of Neil!
A falling firmament of rain the heavens were pouring
    down ;
They heeded not the drowning heavens, nor yet the
    foeman's frown :
Forward they strained with hearts a-fire, and gallantly
    they toiled
Till darkness fell upon them : then the Moon rose up
    and smiled.
A little thing ! and yet it seemed at such a time to
    come
Just like a proud and mournful smile from the very
    heart of Home.

That night they halted in a snipe-swamp; hungry,
    cold, and drencht;
With hearts that kept the blitheness of brave men
    that never blencht.
Thro' flooding nullah, slushy sand, onward they strode
    again,
Ere Dawn, a wingéd glory, alit upon the burnisht
    rain,
And mists up-gathered sullenly along the rear of
    flight,
Slowly as beaten Bellooches might lounge from out
    the fight.
Then heaven grew like inverted hell; a blazing vault
    of fire!
The Sun pursuing pitiless, to bring the brain-strokes
    nigher;
With white heat blinding in their front, and burning
    down all day,
Intently as the eyes of Death a-feeding on his prey.

All the day long, and every day, with patience con-
    quering pain,
Our good and gallant fellows with one purpose for-
    ward strain;
For there is that within each heart nothing but death
    can stop;
They hurry on, and hurry on, and hurry till they drop;

Trying to save the remnant; reach the leaguered
    place in time
To grasp, with red-wet slaughtering hands, the
    workers of this crime.
They think of all the dead that float adown the
    Ganges' waters:
Those noble Englishmen of ours; their gentle wives
    and daughters!
Of Fire and Madness broken loose, and doing deeds
    most pitiful;
And then of vengeance dealt out by the choaked and
    blackened city-full.

They think of those poor things that climb each little
    eminence;
As, from the deluge of the dark, when day is going
    hence,
The sheep will huddle up the hill, and gather there
    forlorn;
So gather they in this dread night, to wait the far-off
    morn.
Or, crouching in the jungle, they look up in Nature's face,
To find she has no heart, for all her reptilinear grace!
Each leaf a sword, or prickly spear, or lifted jagged
    knife!
No shields of shelter like our leaves; but threatening
    human life,

With ominous gouts of blood ;. and there the roots go
    writhing round,   [derground.
Like curses coiled upon the spring, that rest not un-

They find sure tokens all the day ! and starting from
    their dream
At night, they hear the Pariah dogs that howl by
    Ganges stream,
Knowing the waters bear their freight of corpses stiff
    and stark,   [the dark ;
Scenting the footfalls on the air, as Death comes down
Only the Lotus with ripe lips, and arms caressing clings.
The silence swarms with ghastly thoughts ; each
    sound with ghastly things.
There, stands the plough i' the furrow ; there the
    villagers have flown !
There, Fire ran dancing over roofs that underfoot
    went down !
There, Renaud hung his dangling dead, with but
    short time for shrift,
He caught them on their way to hell, and gave them
    there a lift.

They saw the first sight of their foe as the fourth
    dawn grew red ;
Twenty miles to breakfast marched ; and had to fight
    instead.

The morning smiled on arms up-piled, and weary
     way-worn men,
But soon the assembly sounded, and they sprung to
     arms again ;
The heaviest hearts up-leaping light, as flames that
     tread on air.
The Rebel line bore down as they had caught us
     unaware ;
But Maude dasht forward with his guns, over the
     sandy mire,
And little did they relish our bright rain of rifle fire :
Quickly the onward way was ploughed, with heaps on
     either hand ;
They broke the foe, then broke their fast, that daunt-
     less little band.

Again they felt our withering fire, by Pandoo Nuddee
     stream ;
Again they feared the crashing charge, and fled the
     vengeful gleam :
Small loss was his in battle when the Conqueror
     lookt around ;   [wound.
But many fell from weariness, and died without a
Soft, whispering flowery secrets, came a low wind of
     the west
That eve, like breath made balmy with the sweet love
     in the breast ;

Breathing its freshness thro' the groves of Mango and
    of Palm ;
But the sweetest thing that wind could bring was
    slumber's holy balm,
To bless them for the morrow, and give strength for
    them to cope
With those ten thousand men that stood betwixt
    them and their hope.

It must have been a glorious sight to see them as they
    went,
With veteran valour steady; sure of proud accom-
    plishment,
When Havelock bade his line advance, and the High-
    landers swept on ;
Each one at heart a thousand ; a thousand men as one ;
Linked in their beautiful proud line across the broken
    lands,
Straight on ! they never paused to lift the weapon
    in their hands ;   [cloud,
Silent, compact and resolute, charged as a thunder-
That burst, and wrapt the dead and living in one
    smoky shroud ;
One volley of Defiance ! one wild cheer ! and through
    the smoke,
They flasht ! and all the battle into flying fragments
    broke.

When night came down they lay there, gashed all
    over, side by side,
The grey old warrior, and the youth, his Mother's
    darling pride!
Rolled with the rebel in the dust, and grim in bloody
    death;
And over all the mist arose, dank as the graveyard's
    breath.
But light of heart we took the hill, and very proud
    that night
Was Havelock of his noble men, and Cawnpore was
    in sight.
The men had neither food nor tent, but the red road
    was won:
And very proud were they to hear their General's
    " Well done; "
Not knowing how their triumph-cheer had rung a
    fatal knell;
Or what that wondrous wretch had done who has no
    match in hell.

CAWNPORE.

CAWNPORE was ghastly silent, as into it they stepped;
There stood the blackened Ruin that the brave old
    Soldier kept!
Where strained each ear for the English cheer, and
    stretcht the wan wide eyes,
Thro' all that awful night to see the signal rocket rise;
No tramp, no cheer of Brothers near; no distant
    cannon's boom;
Nothing but Death goes to and fro betwixt the glare
    and gloom.
The living remnant try to hold their bit of blood-
    stained ground;
Dark gaps continual in their midst; the dead all
    lying round;
And saddest corpses still are those that die and do
    not die;
With just a little glimmering light of life to show
    them by.

Each drop of water cost a wound to fetch it from the
    well;
The father heard his crying child and went, but surely
    fell.

They had drunk all their tears, and now dry agony
    drank their blood;
The sand was killing in their souls; the wind a fiery
    flood;   [wold!
Oh, for one waft of heather-breath from off a Scottish
One shower that makes our English leaves smile
    greener for its gold!
Then life drops inward from the eyes; turns upward
    with last prayer,
To look for its deliverance; the only way lies there!
And then triumphant Treachery made leap each
    trusting heart,
Like some poor Bird called from the nest, up-poising
    for the dart.

" Come, let us pray," their Chaplain said. No other
    boon was craved:
No pleading word for mercy sued; no face the white
    flag waved;
But all grasped hands and prayed, till peace their
    souls serenely filled;
Then like our noble Martyrs, there they stood up,
    and were killed.
Only one saved!
        He led our soldiers to the house of blood;
An eager, panting, cursing crew! but stricken there
    they stood

In silence that was breathlessness of vengeance
  infinite ;
A-many wept like women who were fiercest in the
  fight :
There grew a look in human eyes as tho' a wild
  beast came
Up in them at that scent of blood and glared devouring flame.

All the Babes and Women butchered! all the dear
  ones dead ;
The story of their martyrdom in lines of awful red !
The blood-black floor, the clotted gore, fair tresses,
  fierce sword-dints ;
Last message-scrawl upon the wall, and tiny finger-
  prints :
Gathered in one were all strange sights of horror and
  despair,
That make the vision blood-shot, freeze the life, or
  lift the hair.
Faces to faces flasht hell-fire ! O, but they felt
  'twould take
The very cup of God's own wrath, that terrible thirst
  to slake :
For many a day " Cawnpore" was hissed, and, at its
  word of guilt,   [the hilt.
The slaying sword went merciless right, ruddy to

There came a time we caught them, with a vast and
    whelming wave,
And in their grand Secunder Bagh, we made a
    bloody grave!
Once more the Highlanders pressed on with nervous,
    springy tread,
And Peel was there with his big guns, and Campbell
    at their head:
A spring of daring madness! and they leapt upon
    their prey   [a day.
With hungry hearts on fury fed, for many and many
For hours and hours, they slew, and slew, the devils
    in their den:
" Ye wreaked your will on women weak, now try it
    with strong men."
The blood that cried to heaven long in vapours from
    our slain,
Fell hot and fast upon their heads in a rich ruddy rain.

That day we made their delicate white marble glow
    and swim ;
There rose a cry like hell from out a slaughter great
    and grim :
And as they claspt their hands and sued for mercy
    where they fell,
One last sure thrust was given for that red and
    writhing Well.

And there was joy in every heart, and light in
 every eye,
To see the traitor hordes that fled, make a last stand
 to die!
While from the big wide wounds, like snakes, the
 runlets crawled along
And stole away ; the reptiles who had done the cruel
 wrong !
A terrible reprisal for each precious drop they spilled.
Seventeen hundred coward killers there were bravely
 killed.

The Relief.

England's unseen, dead Sorrow doth a visible Angel
    rise ;
The sword of justice in her hand ; Revenge looks
    thro' her eyes :
Stern with the purpose in her soul right onward
    hastens she,
Like one that bears the doom of worlds, with venge-
    ful majesty ;
Sombre, superb, and terrible, before them still she
    goes !
And tho' they lessen day by day, they deal such echo-
    ing blows,
That still dilating with success, still mightier grows
    that band,
Till in the place of hundreds, ten thousand seem to
    stand.
With arms that weary not at work, they bear our
    victor flag,
To plant it high on hills of dead, a torn and bloody
    rag.

And Lucknow lies before them now, with all its
    pomp unrolled ;
Against the smiling sapphire, gleam her tops of
    lighted gold.
Each royal wall is fretted all with frostwork and
    with fire,
A glory of colours jewel-rich, that makes a splendour-
    pyre,
As wave on wave the wonder breaks, the pointed
    flames burn higher ;   [spire ;
On dome of mosque and minaret, on pinnacle and
Fairy creations, seen mid-air, that in their pleasaunce
    wait,
Like wingéd creatures sitting just outside their
    heaven-gate.
The City in its beauty lies, with flowers about her feet ;
Green fields, and goodly gardens, make so foul a
    thing seem sweet.

The Trumpet rings out for the march with utterance
    golden-grand,
A sound that shivers to the heart of Havelock's little
    band,
And makes their spirits thrill as leaves are thrilled in
    some wild wind ;
Hunger and heartache, weariness and wounds, all left
    behind.

Their sufferings all forgotten now, as in the ranks
        they form ;   [storm.
And every man in stature rose to wrestle with that
All silent! what was in their hearts could not be said
        in words ;
With faces set for Lucknow, ground to sharpness,
        keen as swords !
A tightning twitch all over! a grim glistening in
        the eye,
" Forward !" and on their way they strode to dare,
        and do, and die.

Hope whispers at the ear of some, that they shall
        meet again,
And clasp their long-lost darlings, after all the toil
        and pain ;
A-many know that they will sleep to-night among
        the slain ;
And many a cheek will bloom no more for all the
        tearful rain :
And some have only vengeance ; but to-day 'tis
        bitter sweet ;
And there goes Havelock ! his aim too lofty for defeat ;
With steady tramp the column treads, true as the
        firm heart's-beat ;
Upon its headlong murderous march for that long
        fatal street.

All ready to win a soldier's grave, or do the daring
    deed!
But not a man that fears to die for England in her
    need.

The masked artillery raked the road, and plough'd
    them front and flank ;   [rank ;
Some gallant fellow every step was stricken from the
But, as he staggered, in his place another sternly
    stepped ;
And, firing fast as they could load, their onward
    way they kept.
Now, give them the good bayonet ! with England's
    fiercest foes,
Strong arm, cold steel will do it, in the wildest,
    bloodiest close :   [ridge,
And now their bayonets abreast go sparkling up the
And with a thrilling cheer they take the guns, and
    clear the bridge.
One good home-thrust ! and surely, as the dead in
    doom are sure,
They send them where the British cheer can trouble
    them no more.

The fire is biting bitterly ; onward the battle rolls ;
And Death is glaring at them, from ten thousand
    hiding holes ;

Death stretches up from earth to heaven, spreading
    his darkness round ;
Death piles the heaps of helplessness face downward
    to the ground ;
Death flames from deadly ambuscades, where all was
    still and dark ;
Death swiftly speeds on whizzing wings the bullets to
    their mark ;
Death from the doors and windows, all around and
    overhead,
Darts, with his cloven fiery tongues, incessant, quick,
    and red :
Death everywhere, Death in all sounds, and, thro'
    the smoky seeth,
Victory beckons at the end of long dark lanes of
    death.

Another charge, another cheer, another battery won !
And in a whirlwind of fierce fire the fight goes roar-
    ing on.   [fast,
Into the very heart of hell, with comrades falling
Thro' all that tempest terrible, the glorious remnant
    passed.
No time to help a dear old friend : but where the
    wounded fell,
They knew it was all over, and they lookt a last
    farewell.

And dying eyes, slow setting in a cold and stony stare,
Turned upward, see a map of murder scribbled on
  the air
With crossing flames; and others read their fiery
  fearful fate,
In dark, swart faces waiting for them, almost white
  with hate.

O, proudly men will march to death, when Havelock
  leads them on:
Thro' all the storm he sat his horse as he were cut in
  stone!
But now his look grows dark; his eye lightens with
  quicker flash:
" On, for the Residency, we must make a last brave
  dash."
And on dasht Highlander and Sikh thro' a sea of fire
  and steel,
On, with the lion of their strength, our first in glory,
  Niel!
It seemed the face of heaven grew black, so close it
  held its breath,
Through all the glorious agony of that long march
  of death.   [spread thy shield!
The round shot tears, the bullets rain; O God, out-
Put forth thy red right arm, for them! thy sword of
  sharpness wield.

One wave breaks forward on the shore, and one falls
    helpless back :
Again they club their wasted strength, to fight like
    " Hell-fire Jack."
And, still as fainter grows the fire of that intrepid
    band,   [hand.
Again they grasp the bayonet as 'twere Salvation's
They leap the broad, deep trenches, rush thro' arch-
    ways streaming fire ;
Every step some brave heart bursts, heaving deliver-
    ance nigher :
" I'm hit," cries one, " you'll take me on your back,
    my comrade, I
Should like to see their bonny white faces once be-
    fore I die ;
My body may save you from the shot."
                 His comrade bore him on :
But, ere they reacht the Bailie Guard, the longing
    soul was gone.

And now the Gateway was in sight ; the last grim
    moment came.
One moment makes immortal ! dead or living, end-
    less fame !   [thrilled ;
They heard the voice of fiery Niel, that like a trumpet
" Push on my men, 'tis getting dark :" he sat where
    he was killed.

Another frantic surge of life, and plunging o'er the
    bar,   [of war,
Right into harbour bursting goes their whirling wave
And breaks in mighty thunders of reverberating
    cheers,   [tears.
Then dances on in frolic foam of kisses, blessings,
Stabbed by mistake, one native cries with the last
    breath he draws,
" Welcome, my friends, never you mind, it's all for
    the good cause."

How they had leaned and listened, as the battle
    sounded nigher ;
How they had strained their eyes to see them coming
    crown'd with fire !
Till in the flashing street they heard them breathing
    bloody breath,
And then the English faces came white from the
    clouds of death ;
And iron grasp met tender clasp ; wan weeping
    women fold
Their dear Deliverers, down whose long rough beards
    the big tears rolled.
Another such a meeting will not be on this side
    heaven!
The little wine they have hoarded, to the last drop
    shall be given

To those who, in their mortal need, fought on thro'
    fearful odds,
Bled for them, reacht them, saved them, less like
    men than glorious gods.

DEATH OF HAVELOCK.

THE Warrior may be ripe for rest, and laurelled with
    great deeds,
But till their work be done, no rest for those whom
    God yet needs :
Whether in rivers of ruin their onward way they tear,
Or healing waters trembling with the beauty that
    they bear ;
Blasting or blessing they must on : on, on, for ever on !
Divine unrest is in their breast, until their work be
    done.
Nor is it all a pleasant path the sacred band must
    tread,
With life a summer holiday, and death a downy bed !
They wear away with noble use, they drink the
    tearful cup ;
And they must bear the bitter cross who go with
    Christ to sup.

Each day his face grew thinner, and sweeter, saint-
    lier grew
The smiling soul that every day was burning keenlier
    through.

And higher, each day higher, did the life-flame
    heavenward climb.

Like sad sweet sunshine up the wall, that for the
    sunset time

Still watches; and the signal that shall call it hence
    is given;

Even so his spirit kept the watch, till beckoned home
    to heaven.

His work was done, his eyes with peace were soft
    and satisfied;

War-worn and wasted, in the arms of Victory he died.

" Havelock 's dead," and darkness fell on every up-
    turned face;

The shadow of an Angel passing from its earthly place.

They laid it low, the old grey head, not only grey
    with years;

It had been bowed in Sorrow's lap and silvered with
    her tears;

Our England may not crown it, with her heart too
    full for speech;

The hand that draws into the dark, hath borne it
    beyond reach.

The eyes of far-away heaven-blue, with such keen
    lustre lit,

As they could pierce the dark of death, and, star-like,
    fathom it,

They may not swim with sweetness as the happy
    Children run
To welcome home the Reaper, when the weary day
    is done!
How would the tremulous radiance round the old
    man's mouth have smiled;
Our good grey-headed hero, with the heart of a little
    child.

In grandest strength he fell, full-length; and now our
    hero climbs
To those who stood up in their day and spoke with
    after times:
There on the battlements of Heaven, they watch us,
    looking back
To see the blessing flow for those who follow in their
    track.
He smileth from his heaven now; the Martyr with
    his palm;   [calm.
The weary warrior's tired life is crown'd with starry
On many sailing thro' the storm another star shall
    shine,
And they shall look up thro' the night and conquer
    at the sign.
In the red pass of peril, with a fame shall never dim,
Died Havelock, the Good Soldier; who would not die
    like him?

Honour to Henry Havelock! tho' not of kingly blood,
He wore the double royalty of being great and good.
He rose and reacht the topmost height; our Hero
    lowly born:
So from the lowly grass hath grown the proud em-
    battled Corn!
He rose up in our cruel need, and towering on he trod;
Bearing his brow to battle bold, as humbly to his God.
He did his work nor thought of nations ringing with
    his name,
He walkt with God, and talkt with God, nor cared
    if following Fame   [ground;
Should find him toiling in the field, or sleeping under-
Nor did he mind what resting-place, with heaven em-
    bracing round.

When swarming hell had broken bounds, he showed
    us how to stand
With rootage like the Palm amidst the maddest whirl
    of sand;
Undaunted while the swarthy storm around him
    swirled and swirled,
A winding sheet of all white life! a wild Sahara world!
The drowning waves closed over him, lost to all
    human view,
But, like an arrow straight from God, he cleft their
    twelve hosts through.

No swerving as he walkt along the rearing earth-
    quake ridge;
He made a way for Victory, his body was her bridge.
Grand in the mouths of men his fame along the cen-
    turies runs;
Women shall read of his great deed and bear heroic
    sons.

He leant a trusting hand on heaven, a gentle heart
    on home;
In secret he grew ready, ere the Judgment hour was
    come.
In darkest days of duty he had seen God's goodness
    shown;
And now, in all his beauty sees the King upon his
    throne!
Some Angel-Mute had led him thro' his trial's thorny
    ways,
Till, on a sudden, lo, he stood, full in the glory's blaze.
Aloud, for all the world to hear, God called his ser-
    vant's name,
And led him forth, where all might see, upon the
    heights of fame.
His arch of life, suspended as it sprang, in heaven
    appears,
Our bow of promise o'er the storm, seen thro' re-
    joicing tears.

Joy to old England! she has stuff for storm-sail and
　　　for stay.
While she can breed such heroes, in her quiet, homely
　　　way:
Such martial souls that go with grim, war-figured
　　　brows pulled down,
As men that are resolved to bear Death's heavy, iron
　　　crown.
So long as she has sons like these, no foe shall make
　　　her bow,
While Ocean washes her white feet; Heaven kisses
　　　her fair brow.
Her beauty high and starlike in its splendour, hath
　　　not fled;
Her bravery high and warlike is not vanisht, is not
　　　dead:
War blows away the ashes gray, and kindles at the core,
Live sparkles of such sacred fire as glowed on Marston
　　　Moor.

Thank God for all our heroes, who so wondrously
　　　have done!　　　　　　　　　　　　　　　[son:
Thank God for men like Havelock, and mighty Nichol-
Hodgeson, of Hodgeson's Horse, who slew the
　　　guiltiest; noble Niel;
And he o' the good Ship Shannon, our beloved Cap-
　　　tain Peel!

If India's fate had rested on each single saviour soul,
They would have kept their grasp of it till we regained
   the whole.
One fighter never would give in, thro' all his fearless
   part:
One fortress they could never win: 'twas the true
   English heart.
The Lightnings of that bursting Cloud, which were
   to blast our might,
But served to shew its majesty clear in the sterner
   light.

Our England towers up beautiful with her dilating form.
To greater stature in the strife, and glory in the
   storm:
Her wrath's great wine-press trodden on so many
   vintage fields,
With crush and strain, and press of pain, a ripened
   spirit yields,
To warm us in our winter, when the times are coward
   and cold.
And work divinely in young veins; bring boyhood to
   the old.
Behold her flame from field to field in Victory's
   chariot wheels.
Till to its den, bleeding to death, Rebellion backward
   reels.

Her Martyrs are aveng'd! ye may search that In-
        dian land,
And scarcely find a single soul of all the bloody band.

We've many a nameless hero lying in his unknown
        grave,
Their life's gold fragment gleaming but a sunfleck on
        the wave.
But rest you unknown, noble dead! our living are
        one hand
Of England's power; but, with her dead she grasps
        into the land.
In many a country they sleep crown'd, her conquer-
        ing, faithful dead ;
They pave her path where shines her sun of empire
        overhead ;
And where their blood has turned to bloom, our
        England's Rose is red :
They circle in a glorious ring, with which the world
        is wed.   [and sod,
For us the flower of our race makes quick the sand
And there, as here, amid our dead, we build our
        Church to God.

Your Brother Willie, boy, was one of Havelock's little
        band :   [Land.
My Son! my beautiful brave Son, lies in that Indian

They buried him by the way-side where he bowed him
    down to die,
While Homeward in its eastern pomp the Triumph
    passed him by.
And even yet mine eyes are wet, but 'tis with that
    proud tear
A great grand feeling in its front doth like a jewel
    wear.
I see him! on his forehead shines the conqueror's
    burning crest,
And God's own cross of Victory is on his martial
    breast.
I should have liked to have felt him near, when these
    old eyes are dim,
But gave him to our England; she had greater need
    of him.

THE NORSEMAN.

A SWARTHY strength, with face of light,
As dark sword-iron is beaten bright:
A brave frank look, with health a-glow,
Bonny blue eyes and open brow;
His friend he welcomes heart-in-hand,
But foot to foot his foe must stand;
A man who will face to his last breath
The sternest facts of life and death:
  This is the daring Norseman.

The wild wave-motion, weird and strange,
Rocks in him: seaward he must range.
For life is just a mighty lust
To wear away with use, not rust.
Though bitter wintry cold the storm,
The fire within him keeps him warm.
Kings quiver at his flag unfurled:
The sea-king's master of the world:
  Conquering comes the Norseman.

He hides, at heart of his rough life,
A world of sweetness for the wife:

From his rude breast a babe may press
Soft milk of human tenderness,
Make his eyes water, his heart dance,
And sunrise in his countenance :
In merry mood his ale he quaffs
By firelight, and his jolly heart laughs;
    The blithe great-hearted Norseman.

But when the battle-trumpet rings,
His soul's a war-horse clad with wings !
He drinks delight in with the breath
Of battle and the dust of death !
The axes redden, spring the sparks,
Blood-radiant grow the grey mail-sarks :
Such blows might batter, as they fell,
Heaven's gates, or burst the booms of hell :
    So fights the fearless Norseman.

The Norseman's King must stand up tall ;
A head that could be seen o'er all ;
Mainmast of Battle ! when the plain
Grew miry red with bloody rain ;
And grip his weapon for the fight,
Until his knuckles all grew white !
Their banner-staff he bears is best
If double handful for the rest,
    When "follow me" cries the Norseman.

E

Valiant and true, as Sagas tell,
The Norseman hated lies like hell;
Hardy from cradle to the grave,
'Twas their religion to be brave;
Great silent fighting men, whose words
Were few, soon said, and out with swords!
One, saw his heart cut from his side,
Living—and smiled; and smiling, died!
    The unconquerable Norseman.

They swam the flood, they strode in flame,
Nor quailed when the Valkyrie came
To kiss the chosen for her charms,
With " Rest, my hero, in mine arms."
Their spirits through a grim wide wound,
The Norse doorway to Heaven found.
And borne upon the battle-blast,
Into the Hall of Heroes passed:
    And there was crowned the Norseman.

The Norseman wrestled with old Rome
For Freedom in our island home:
He taught us how to ride the sea,
With hempen bridle, horse of tree.
His spirit stood with Robin Hood,
By Freedom in the merry green wood,

When William ruled the English land,
With cruel heart and bloody hand;
    For freedom fights the Norseman.

Still in our race the Norse king reigns,
His best blood beats along our veins;
With his old glory we can glow,
And surely steam where he could row.
Is danger stirring? Up from sleep
Our war-dog wakes, his watch to keep;
Stands with our banner over him,
True as of old, and stern and grim;
    Come on, you'll find the Norseman.

When swords are gleaming you shall see
The Norseman's face flash gloriously,
With look that makes the foeman reel:
His mirror from of old was steel.
And still he wields, in battle's hour,
That old Thor's hammer of Norse power;
Strikes with a desperate arm of might,
And at the last tug turns the fight:
    For never yields the Norseman.

OLD KING HAKE.

Got by the Sea on a rocky coast
 Was old King Hake;
Where inner fire and outer frost
 Brave virtue make!
He was a hero in the old
 Blood-letting days;
An iron hero of Norse mould,
 And warring ways.
He lived according to the light
 That lighted him;
Then strode into the eternal night,
 Resolved and grim.
His grip was stern for free sword play,
 When men were mown;
His feet were roughshod for the day
 Of treading down.
When angry, out the blood would start
 With old King Hake;
Not sneak in dark caves of the heart,
 Where curls the snake,
And secret Murder's hiss is heard
 Ere the deed be done.

He wove no web of wile and word;
    He bore with none.
When sharp within its sheath asleep
    Lay his good sword,
He held it royal work to keep
    His kingly word.
A man of valour, bloody and wild,
    In Viking need;
And yet of firelight feeling mild
    As honey-mead.

Once in his youth, from farm to farm,
    Collecting scatt,
He gathered gifts and welcomes warm;
    And one night sat,
With hearts all happy for his throne—
    Wishing no higher—
Where peasant faces merrily shone
    Across the fire.
Their Braga-bowl was handed round
    By one fair girl:
The Sea-King lookt and thought, "I've found
    My hidden pearl."
Her wavy hair was golden fair,
    With sunbeams curled;
Her eyes clear blue as heaven, and there
    Lay his new world.

He drank out of the mighty horn,
    Strong, stinging stuff;
Then wiped his manly mouth unshorn
    With hand as rough,
And kissed her; drew her to his side,
    With loving mien,
Saying, " If you will make her a Bride,
    I'll make her a Queen."
And round her waist she felt an arm,
    For in those days
A waist could feel : 'twas lithe and warm,
    And wore no stays.
" How many brave deeds have you done ? "
    She asked her wooer,
Counting the arm's gold rings : they won
    One victory more.
The blood of joy looked rich and red
    Out of his face ;
And to his smiling strength he wed
    Her maiden grace.
'Twas thus King Hake struck royal root
    In homely ground ;
And healthier buds with goodlier fruit
    His branches crowned.

But Hake could never bind at home
    His spirit free ;

It grew familiar with the foam
  Of many a sea;
A rare good blade whose way was rent
  In many a war,
And wore no gem for ornament
  But notch and scar.
In day of battle and hour of strife,
  Cried Old King Hake:
" Kings live for honour, not long life."
  Then would he break
Right through their circle of shields, to reach
  Some chief of a race
That never yielded ground, but each
  Died in his place.
There the old Norseman towered tall
  Above the rest
A head and shoulders, like King Saul;
  They saw his crest
Toss, where the war-wave reared, and rode
  O'er mounds of dead,
And where the battle-dust was trod
  A miry red.
For Odin, in the glad wide blue
  Of heaven, would laugh
With sunrise, and the ruddy dew
  Of slaughter quaff.

But, 'twas the grandest gallant show
    To see him sit,
With his Long-Serpent all aglow,
    And steering it
For the hot heart of fiercest fight.
    A grewsome shape!
The dragon-head rose. glancing bright.
    And all agape;
Over the calm blue sea it came
    Writhingly on,
As half in sea, and half in flame,
    It swam, and shone.
The sunlit shields link scale to scale
    From stem to stern,
Over the steersman's head the tail
    Doth twist and burn.
With oars all moved at once, it makes
    Low hoverings;
Half walks the water, and half takes
    The air with wings.

The war-horns bid the fight begin
    With death-grip good:
King Hake goes at the foremost, in
    His Bare-Sark mood.
A twelvemonth's taxes spent in spears
    Hurled in an hour!

But in that host no spirit fears
 The hurtling shower.
And long will many a mother and wife
 Wait, weary at home,
Ere from that mortal murderous strife
 Their darlings come.

Hake did not seek to softly die,
 With child and wife :
He bore his head in death as high
 As in his life.
Glittering in eye, and grim in lip,
 He bade them make
Ready for sailing his War-Ship,
 That he, King Hake,
The many-wounded, grey, and old,
 His day being done,
He, the Norse warrior, brave and bold,
 Might die like one.
And chanting some old battle-song,
 Thrilling and weird,
His soul vibrating, shook his long
 Majestic beard.
The gilded battle-axe, still red,
 In his right hand ;
With shield on arm, and helm on head,
 They helpt him stand,

And girded him with his good sword ;
    And so attired,
With his dead warriors all aboard,
    The ship he fired,
And lay down with his heroes dead,
    On deck to die ;
Still singing, drooped his grey old head,
    With face to sky.
The wind blew seawards ; gloriously
    The death-pyre glowed ;
On his last Viking voyage he
    Triumphing rode :
Floating afar between the Isles,
    To his last home,
Where open-armed Valhalla smiles,
    And bids him come.
There, as a sinking sunset dies
    Down in the west,
The fire went out ; the rude heart lies
    At rest—at rest,
And sleeping in its ocean bed,
    That burial-place
Most royal for the kingly dead
    O' the old sea-race !
So the Norse noble of renown,
    With his stern pride,
That flaming crown of death pulled down.
    And so he died.

GARIBALDI.

HE is the Helper that Italy wanted
   To free her from fetters and cerements quite :
His is the great heart no dangers have daunted ;
   His is the true hand to finish the fight.
Way, for a Man of the kingliest nature !
Scope, for a soul of the high Roman stature !
     His great deeds have crown'd him ;
     His heroes are round him ;
On, on Garibaldi, for Freedom and Right.

To brave battle-music up goes the smoke-curtain ;
   A Country arises, all one should he call :
The sound of his trumpet is never uncertain ;
   He fights for his Cause till it conquer or fall.
His chariot wheels do not spin without biting ;
And far better pointed for Freedom's red writing—
     His Rifles and Guns—
     Than their politic pens ;
Garibaldi, my Hero, best Man of them all.

When he sail'd up our river, the frank hearty Seaman,
　　We saw how an English soul smiled from his face:
For Italy's saviour we knew it was the man,
　　All hero, no matter what garb, or what place.
And we prayed he might have one more grip that
　　　was glorious!
Prophesied he should be leader victorious
　　　　Of Italy, free
　　　　From the Alps to the sea;
Now breathless we watch while he runs the great
　　　race.

Fierce out of torment his fighters have risen,
　　Shouting from hell where they tortured them dumb;
Maimed from old battle-fields, mad from the prison,
　　Suddenly, strange as Cloud-armies, they come;
With mouths that can shut like the Eagle's beak
　　　clasping;
With hands that will grip like a bower-anchor grasping;
　　　　The flying foe feels,
　　　　When they're close at his heels,
That Death and the Devil are bringing his doom.

Not only living! but dead men are fighting
　　For him! thus with few he can fight the great host;
For each one they see an unseen foe is smiting;
　　Over each head an avenging white ghost!

All the young Martyrs they murdered by moonlight ;
All the dark deeds of blood done in the noonlight,
  Shall make their hearts reel
  With a shudder, and kneel
To lay down their arms and give all up for lost.

They tell the wild tales of him, gathered together,
 Turn pale at his shadow in midst of their speech ;
For down he swoops on them, like hawk on the heather,
 Strikes home with sure aim, and up-soars beyond
  reach.
Or he sweeps all before him with whirling blade
  reeking ;
They fly helter-skelter, for shelter run shrieking,
  As waves wild and white,
  Driven mad with affright,
Are dasht into foam as they hide up the beach.

Watching o' nights in the cold, he remembers
 The homes of his love in their ashes laid low ;
And hot in his heart Vengeance rakes up the embers,
 To warm her old hands at the wrathful red glow.
He has had torn from him all that was nearest ;
He has seen murdered his darlings the dearest ;
  With all this and more,
  To the heart's crimson core
He kindles! and all flashes out on the Foe.

No Peace, Garibaldi, till Italy, stronger
  Shall sit with free nations, majestic, serene;
And meet them as lovers may meet when no longer
  The cold corse of one that was dead lies between.
For this, God was with you when perils were round
    you;
For this, the fire smote you not, floods have not
  drown'd you;
    Their Sword and their Shot,
    Have harmed you not,
And your Purpose croucht long for its spring un-
  seen.

On, with our British hearts all beating true to you;
  All keeping time to the march of the brave!
I would to God we might cut our way thro' to you,
  Gallantly breasting the stormiest wave.
Would the old Lion could leap in to greet you,
Just as our free blood is leaping to meet you,
    Stand by your side
    In his terrible pride,
Mighty to shield, as You're daring to save.

Long was the night of her kneeling; but surely
  Shall Italy rise to her queenliest height.
Many a time has the battle gone sorely,
  To make the last triumph more signal and bright.

Her foes shall be swept from her path like the stubble,
For now is *their* day of down-treading and trouble;
    God tires of old Rome!
    Venetia cries "Come."
On, on Garibaldi, for Freedom and Right.

SIR RICHARD GRENVILLE'S LAST FIGHT.

Our second Richard Lion-Heart,
    In days of great Queen Bess,
He did this deed of righteous rage,
    And true old nobleness;
With wrath heroic that was nurst
To bear the fieriest battle-burst;
When willing foes should wreak their worst.

Signalled the English Admiral,
    " Weigh or cut Anchors."   For
A Spanish Fleet bore down in all
    The majesty of war,
Athwart our tack for many a mile;
As there we lay off Florez Isle;
Our crews half sick; all tired of toil.

Eleven of our twelve ships escaped.—
    Sir Richard stood alone!
Though they were three-and-fifty-sail—
    A hundred men to one,
The old Sea-Rover would not run,
So long as he had man or gun;
But he could die when all was done.

" The Devil has broken loose, my lads,
　　" In shape of Popish Spain;
" And we must sink him in the sea,
　　" Or hound him home again ;
" Now you old Sea-dogs, show your paws!
" Have at them tooth, and nail, and claws."
And then his long, bright blade he draws.

The deck was cleared, the Boatswain blew ;
　　The grim sea-lions stand,
The death-fires lit in every eye ;
　　The burning match in hand :
With mail of glorious intent
All hearts were clad ; and in they went,
A force that cut through where 'twas sent.

" Push home, my hardy Pikemen ;
　　For we play a desperate part ;
To-day, my Gunners, let them feel
　　The pulse of England's heart !
They shall remember long that we
Once lived ; and think how shamefully
We shook them ! one to fifty-three."

With face of one who cheerly goes
　　To meet his doom that day,

Sir Richard sprang upon his foes ;
    The foremost gave him way ;
His round shot smasht them thro' and thro' ;
The great white splinters fiercely flew ;
And madder grew his fighting few.

They clasp the little Ship Revenge,
    As in the arms of fire ;
They run aboard her, six at once ;
    Hearts beat and guns leap higher :
Through bloody gaps the Boarders swam ;
But still our English stay the storm ;
The bulwark in their breast is firm.

Ship after Ship, like broken waves
    That wash up on a rock,
Those mighty galleons fall back foiled,
    And shattered from the shock.
With fire she answers all their blows ;
Again, again in pieces strows
The burning girdle of her foes.

Through all the night the great white storm
    Of worlds in silence rolled ;
Sirius with his sapphire sparkle ;
    Mars in ruddy gold :

Heaven lookt, with stillness terrible,
Down on a fight most fierce and fell;
A Sea transfigured into hell.

Some know not they are wounded
    · Till 'tis slippery where they stand;
Some with their own good blood make fast
    The pike staff to their hand:
Wild faces glow through lurid night,
With sweat of spirit shining bright:
Only the dead on deck turn white.

At daybreak the flame-picture fades,
    In blackness and in blood;
There! after fifteen hours of fight,
    The unconquered Sea-King stood,
Defying all the power of Spain:
Fifteen Armadas hurled in vain;
And fifteen hundred foemen slain.

Around that little Bark Revenge,
    The baffled Spaniards ride
At distance. Two of their good Ships
    Were sunken at her side;
The rest lie round her in a ring,
As round the dying lion-king,
The Dogs, afraid of his death-spring.

Our pikes all broken ; powder spent ;
    Sails, masts to shreds were blown ;
And with her dead and wounded crew
    The ship was going down !
Sir Richard's wounds were hot and deep ;
Then cried he, with a proud, pale lip,
" Ho Gunner, split and sink the ship ;

" Make ready, now my Mariners,
    " To go aloft with me ;
" That nothing to the Spaniard
    " May remain of victory.
" They cannot take us, nor we yield ;
" So let us leave our battle field,
" Under the shelter of God's shield."

They had not heart to dare fulfil
    The stern commander's word :
With bloody hands, and weeping eyes,
    They carried him aboard
The Spaniard's Ship ; and round him stand
The warriors of his wasted band.
Then said he, feeling death at hand,

" Here die I, Richard Grenville,
    With a joyful and quiet mind ;

I reach a Soldier's end ; I leave
    A Soldier's fame behind ;
Who for his Queen and Country fought,
For Honour and Religion wrought,
And died as a true Soldier ought."

Earth never returned a worthier trust,
    For hand of Heaven to take,
Since Arthur's sword, Excalibur,
    Was cast into the lake,
And the King's grievous wounds were dressed,
And healed by weeping Queens who blessed,
And bore him to a valley of rest.

Old Heroes who could grandly do,
    As they could greatly dare ;
A vesture, very glorious,
    Their shining spirits wear,
Of noble deeds. God give us grace,
That we may see such face to face,
In our great day that comes apace.

SIR ROBERT'S SAILOR SON.

Our country hath no need to raise
    The ghosts of glories gone ;
Such heroes dying in our days,
    Still hand the live torch on.
Brave blood as bright a crimson gleams,
    Still burns as goodly zeal ;
The old heroic radiance beams
    In men like William Peel.

With beautiful bravery clothèd on,
    And such high moral grace,
The flash of rare soul-armour shone
    Out of his noble face !
So mild in peace, so stern in war,
    He walkt our English way ;
Just one of Shakespeare's Warriors for
    A weary working day.

His Sailors loved him so on deck ;
    So cheery was his call,
They leapt on land, and in his wake
    Followed him, guns and all.

For, as a battle-brand red-hot,
   His Spirit grew and glowed,
When in his swift war-chariot
   The Avenger rose and rode.

Sleep, Sailor Darling, true and brave,
   With our dead Soldiers sleep!
That so the land you lived to save,
   You shall have died to keep.
You may have wished the dear Sea-blue
   To have folded round your breast;
But God had other work for you,
   And other place of rest.

We might have reacht you with our wreath
   If living; but laid low,
You grow so grand; and after death
   The dearness deepens so!
To have gone so soon, so loved to have died,
   So young to wear that crown,
We think.   Yet with such thrills of pride
   As shake the last tears down.

Our old Norse Fathers speak thro' you;
   Speak with their strange sea-charm,
That sets our hearts a-beating to
   The music of the storm.

There comes a Spirit from the deep
　　The salt wind waves its wings ;
That rouses from our Inland sleep
　　The blood of the old Sea Kings.

God rest you, gallant William Peel,
　　With those whom England leaves
Scattered, while yet she plies her steel,
　　But God gleans up in sheaves.
We'll talk of you on land, a-board,
　　Till Boys shall feel as Men,
And forests of hands clutch at this Sword
　　Death gives us back again.

ONE OF GARIBALDI'S MEN.

A CRIPPLED Child, a weak wan Boy,
    He sat at Mother's side,—
A widowed Mother's gentle joy,
    Her only wealth and pride :—
One of those spirits, sweet and sad,
    That breathe with burthened breath,
Are grave in life, but calmly glad
    Their faces smile in death.

With a weird lustre in his look,
    Over his books he pored,
Like one that, in a secret nook,
    Sharpens a patriot sword.
The story of his country's wrongs
    Made his heart melt in tears ;
The music of her olden songs
    Rang thrilling in his ears.

Oft in his face, white as a corse,
    Brave soldier blood up-springs,

Hot as the warrior leaps to horse,
    When Battle's trumpet rings;
With spirit afloat and blood a-flame,
    Where Freedom's banners wave,
To win a name of glorious fame,
    Or fill a Soldier's grave.

The leal heart of a loving Maid
    Ran over towards him,
Longing with kisses to be stayed
    There at the ruddy brim!
But husht the yearning in her breast,
    Nor murmur made nor moan;
And lookt as she had found the nest,
    But, lo! the Bird was flown.

Suddenly, Freedom's thunder-horn
    The graveyard stillness broke;—
It was the resurrection-morn,
    And Italy awoke!
He felt her majesty and strength
    Lift up his spirit too:
To Manhood he had leapt at length,
    And almost stately grew.

Then came, with all they had to give,
    Each kneeling worshipper:

And he, too, not worth much to live,
    But he could die for her.
The Widow gave her only Child,
    Blessed him, and bade him win;
And outwardly her proud face smiled,
    While dropping tears within.

The General lookt on this young life
    Held out in hands so small!
He could not, for the battle-strife,
    Take the poor Widow's all.
" Poor Child!" he said, " rest you at home
    For the good Mother's sake;
We'll not forget you when we come."
    It made his old heart ache.

'Twas at the close of one great day,
    The Red Shirts raised their cheer,
For Garibaldi came to say,
    " Well done!"   One cried, " I'm here!
And wounded in the battle's brunt."
    " What! hit behind, my child?
But brave men wear their wounds in front."
    And playfully he smiled.

Again, at the Volturno's fight
    The boy led on his band;

Uplifted there on Capua's height,
      He saw the Promised Land,
As Pilgrims see their Mecca rise
      Over the desert's rim ;—
He saw,—possessed it with his eyes!
      Enough, enough for him.

Proud of his Boys, the General rode
      Past faces all a-flame,
And praised them ; and their spirits glowed
      As if from heaven he came.
Then something caught his eye ; he reined
      His horse, stooped like a grand
Old weather-beaten angel, stained
      With battle-smoke, and tanned!

With look more loud than cry or call,
      One staggered from the rest :
" I'm hit once more, my General,—
      And"—pointing to his breast,—
" This time—see !—'tis in the right place."
      His smile was strangely sweet :
He lookt in Garibaldi's face,
      And fell dead at his feet !

HUGH MILLER'S GRAVE.

Before the grim grave closes, let me drop
My few poor flowers upon his Coffin lid !
I loved the man : his taking roughness too
I liked ; it was the Sword-hilt rough with gems.
I loved him living, not with that late love
Which asks for rootage in the dead man's grave,
And must be writ in Marble to endure.
To many he seemed stern, for he could guard
His tongue with his good teeth : to some he showed
Rough as the Holly's lower range of leaves,
His prickly humour all alive with spears :
But if you climbed to the serener height,
You found a life in smooth and shining leaf,
And crowned with calm, and lying nearer heaven.

Low lies the grandest head in all Scotland.
We'll miss him when there's noble work to do !
We'll miss him coming thro' the crowded street,
Like plaided Shepherd from the Ross-shire Hills,
Stalwart and iron-grey and weather-worn ;

His tall head holding up a lonely lamp
Of steadfast thought still burning in his eyes,
Like some masthead-light lonely thro' the night;
His eyes, that rather dreamed than saw, deep-set
In the brow's shadow, looking forward, fixed
On something which we saw not, solemn, strange!

He was a Hero true as ever stept
In the Forlorn Hope of a warring world:
And from opposing circumstance his palm
Drew loftier stature, and a lustier strength.
From the far dreamland height of youthful years
He flung his gage out mid the trampling strife,
And fought his way to it with spirit that cut
Like a scythed chariot, and took up his own.
Once more Childe Roland to the dark tower came,
Saw bright forms beckon on the battlements,
And stormed thro' fighting foes, true steel to steel;
Slow step by step he won his winding way,
And reached the top, and stood up Victor there;
And yet with most brave meekness it was done.
His life-tree fair of leaf, and rich in fruit!
We could not see it mouldering at the heart.
We knew not how in nights of pain he groped,
And groped with bleeding feet down the dark crypts
Of consciousness, to find the buried sense;
When the faint flame of being flickering low,

Made fearful shadows spectral on the walls;
And beckoning terrors muttered in the dark;
Old misery-mongers moaned along the wind;
The lights burned blue as Death were breathing near,
And dead hands seemed to reach and drag him down.
The powers of Evil often have a hand
With human Lots in the dim urn of Fate.

The awful Dark flung over him a pall
Of pain, hot hands of hell were on his eyes,
And Devils drew him thro' the cold night-wind;
But while they held the helpless body bound,
The spirit broke away. That rent was death!
The iron will wherewith he cleft his path
From the stone-quarries to the heights of fame,
Still strove for freedom when the leap was death.

Ay me, poor fellow! would we had but known,
And reacht him in that horror of great gloom,
And caught his hand, and prayed that he would bid
Us kindlier farewell : leave us when 'twas light !

But, never doubt God's Children find their home
By dark as well as day. The life he lived,
And not the death he died, was first in judgment.
It is the writing on the folded scroll
Death sends, and not the seal, that God will judge.

G

I love to think the Spirit of Cowper caught
Hold of his poor weak wandering hands in help,
As at the dark door he in blindness groped.
How it would touch that tender soul to read
The earthly memories written in his face !
Such memories as ope the gates of heaven :
And he who soothed him with last words on earth
Might whisper his first welcome in the heavens,
And lead him thro' cool valleys green where grow
The leaves of healing by the river of life,
Where tears and travel-stains are wiped away,
All troubled thoughts laid in ambrosial rest,
And there is no more pain.

       Then as they bowed
Before His throne who sitteth in the Heavens,
Perchance the pleading Poet prayed that he
Might sit beside him at th' eternal feast.
The fancy flower-like from his coffin grew
Even while I lookt.   He lay as Death did seem
Only a dream he might have dreamed before ;
All peaceful as the face of Sabbath morn :
The meekened witness of another world.
That stern white stillness had a starry touch,
As his last look had caught the first of heaven.
The battle-armour of a soldier soul
Lay battered, but still bright from many blows,
Upon the field ; and such as few could wear.

The ghosts of last year leaves, that last night rose
And rustled in their spectral dance of death,
Are laid and silent in a shroud of snow!
The day is dark above the long dark host!
The sad husht heavens seem choked, but cannot weep!
Many pale faces, many tristful eyes,
With dumb looks pleading for the kindly rain
That comes not when the heart can only cry
With unshed tears, close round his wintry grave!
The lonely men whose lives are still alight
And shining when the tired toilers sleep,
To whom Night brings the larger thoughts like Stars.
I marvel if among them there is one
Who shudders when men speak of such a death
As if they named His—who has longed to pluck
Death's cool hand down upon the burning brain,
But chokes the secret in his heart as though
He crusht a hissing serpent in his hand,
Lest it scream out, and his white face be known!

Ah! come away, for sorrow is a child
That needs no nursing! And all seems so strange.
One last look, and then home to feel and feel
What we have lost; and when from the dark earth
A spring-tide dawn of leaf-light glistens green,
And Nature with her dewfall and her rain
Gives to our grief the last calm tender touch,

And makes the Heartsease grow from out his grave,
In those sweet days when hearts are tenderest
For those who never come back with the flowers,
Upon some balmy Eve so beautiful
We should not wonder if an Angel stood
Suddenly at our side ; the silent march
Of all the beauty culminating thus !
Then let us come, dear friend, and spend an hour—
While Nature kneeleth in all places lowly,
God's blessing resting on a time so holy—
At the communion table of His tomb.

ROBERT BLAKE.

Our Happy Warrior! of a race
   To whom are richly given
Great glory and peculiar grace,
   Because in league with Heaven:
Not that the mortal course they trod
   Was free from briar and thorn!
Who wears the arrow-mark of God,
   The wound must first have borne.

So like a Sailor Saint was he,
   Our Sea-King; grave and sweet
In temper after victory,
   And cheerful in defeat.
And men would leave their quiet home,
   To follow in his wake,
And fight in fire, or float in foam,
   For love of Robert Blake.

Like that drum-head of Zisca's skin,
   Thrills his heroic name;
And how the salt-sea-sparkle in
   Us, flashes at his fame!

His Picture in our heart's best books
　　Still keeps its pride of place,
From which a lofty spirit looks
　　With an unfading face ;

A face as of an Angel who
　　Might live his Boyhood here !
And yet how deadly grand it grew
　　When Wrong drew darkening near.
All ridged and ready trencht for war,
　　The fair frank brow was bent ;
Then flasht, like sudden scimitar,
　　The lion lineament.

Behold him with his gallant band,
　　On leagured Lyme's red beach ;
Shoulder to shoulder see them stand
　　At Taunton in the breach !
Safe through the battle-shocks he went
　　With sword-sweep stern and wide ;
Strode the grim heaps as Death had lent
　　Him his White Horse to ride.

" Give in ! our toils you cannot break ;
　　The Lion is in the net !
Famine fights for us." " No," said Blake,
　　" My boots I have not ate."

He smiled across the bitter cup;
 He gripped his good sword-heft;
"I should not dream of giving up
 While such a meal is left."

Where trumpets blow, and streamers flow,
 Behold him calm and proud,
Bear down upon his bravest foe;
 A bursting thunder-cloud!
Foremost of all the host that strove
 To crowd Death's open door,
In giant mood his way he clove;
 The Man to go before!

And tho' the Battle-lightning blazed;
 The thunders roar and roll;
He to Immortal Beauty raised
 A statue with his soul.
And never did the Greeks of old
 Mirror in marble rare
A Wrestler of so fine a mould;
 An Athlete half so fair.

Homeward the dying Sea-King turns
 From his last famous fight;
For England's dear green hills he yearns,
 And strains his fading sight:

The old cliffs loom out dim and grand,
　　The old War-ship glides on—
With one last wave life tries to land,
　　Falls seaward, and is gone.

With that last leap to touch the coast,
　　He passed into his rest,
And Blake's unwearying arms were crossed
　　For ever on his breast;
And while our England waits and twines
　　For him her latest wreath,
His is a crown of stars that shines
　　From out the dusk of death.

For him no pleasant age of ease
　　To wear what Youth could win;
For him no Children round his knees
　　To get his harvest in.
But with a soul serene he takes
　　Whatever lot may come;
And such a life of labour makes
　　A glorious going home.

Famous old Trueheart, dead and gone,
　　Long shall his glory grow;
He never turned his back upon
　　A friend, nor face from foe.

He made them fear old England's name
    Wherever it was heard ;
He put her proudest foes to shame,
    And God smiled on his Sword.

With lofty courage, loftier love,
    He died for England's sake ;
And mid our loftiest lights above,
    Shines our illustrious Blake !—
And shall shine ! Glory of the West,
    And Beacon for the seas ;
While Britain bares her sailor breast
    To battle or to breeze.

Till she forget her old sea-fame,
    Shall England honour him,
And keep the grave-grass from his name
    Till her old eyes be dim.
And long as free waves folding round,
    Brimful with blessing break,
At heart she holds him, calm and crown'd,
    Immortal Robert Blake.

Great Sailor on the seas of strife ;
    Victor by land and wave ;
Brave liver of a gallant life ;
    Lord of a glorious grave

True Soldier set on earthly hill
As Sentinel of heaven;
A King who keeps his kingdom till
The last award be given.

THE OLD FLAG.

An Emperor babbled in his dreams,—
 Ne'er sleeps the secret in his soul,—
" The Lion is old, and ready he seems
 To draw my Chariot to its goal."
With awful light the Lion's eye
 Began to flame—sublime he stands!
With looks that make the Tyrant try
 To hide his bloody hands.
Thank God, the advancing tide is met!
Thank God, the Old Flag's flying yet.

We love our native land and laws,
 And He would rather we did not!
We are Conspirators because
 We are in our little green grass plot!
But let him follow up his frown,
 Marshal his myriads for the blow;
Those who are doomed to drown must drown;
 The rest we'll take in tow!

In Cherbourg's sight their gallows set
Beside the Old Flag flying yet.

Our Ghost of Greatness hath not fled
　　At crowing of the Gallic Cock;
A foreign Despot's heel shall tread
　　No print upon our English rock.
Here Freedom by the Lion grand
　　Sits safe, and Una-like doth hold
Him gently with her gentle hand;
　　And long as seas enfold,
High on our topmost height firm-set,
We'll keep her Old Flag flying yet.

To Freedom we must aye be true;
　　Our England must be Freedom's home;
For sake of our dead Darlings who
　　Went heavenward crowned with martyrdom.
'Twas she who made us what we are,
　　Throned on our sea-cliffs grey and grand;
Great image of majestic care;
　　Fair Bride of Fatherland!
We do but pay the filial debt
To keep her Old Flag flying yet.

This little Isle is Freedom's Bark
　　That rideth in a perilous path:

Around us one wide sea of dark
   That beats and breaks in stormy wrath.
The Despots drove poor Freedom forth,
   By bloody footprints trackt her road ;—
And homeless, homeless, else on earth
   She takes to her sea-abode !
She turns on us her eyes tear-wet ;
Ah, keep the Old Flag flying yet.

Statesmen have drawn back meek and mute,
   Or pardon begged from bullying foes,
Whene'er a Military boot
   Was stampt upon retreating toes.
They shrink to hear Him at our gates,
   This ominous thing of gloom and gore,
Tho' Revolution for him waits
   At Danger's every door.
But little do we heed his threat !
We keep the Old Flag flying yet.

Over the praying peoples rolled
   The dark tide, and we helpt them not.
Yet, on our lifted hands, behold,
   We cry, behold no bloody spot !
This famous people's heart is sound,
   It fights for all that bleed and smart ;
We—banned above—meet underground,
   Meet in a touch of heart.

We cannot our old fame forget ;
We keep the Old Flag flying yet.

We have a true and tender clasp
    For Freedom's friends where'er their home ;
And for her foes as grim a grasp,
    No matter when or whence they come.
We like that gay light-hearted France
    That into stormy splendour breaks,
When its brave music for the dance
    Of Death the battle makes ;
And foot to foot would proudly set
To keep the Old Flag flying yet.

But what is France ? this cruel Power
    That builds upon her martyred dead,
Whose spirits thicken hour by hour
    The air about its dooméd head ?
This Death-in-Life throned on the grave,
    That in the darkness waits its prey ?
Like Coral-workers neath the wave,
    It dies on reaching day.
The Sun of France hath not thus set,
But, keep the Old Flag flying yet.

France, who hath stood erect and first,
    Will not lie latest in the dust :

Ere long her breath of scorn will burst
   This bubble blown of bloody lust.
Quietly, quietly turns the tide,
   And when this shore lies black and bare,
There shall be no more sea to hide
   The Wrecker's secrets there.
Our lot is cast, our task is set,
To keep the Old Flag flying yet.

Save him ? this Burglar of the night
   Broke into Freedom's sacred shrines !
This Lie uncrowned whene'er the light
   Of merciless next morning shines !
This terror of a land struck dumb,
   Who fed the Furies with brave blood !
We cannot save him when they come
   For his.   Not if we would.
So slippery is the hand blood-wet !
Ah, keep the Old Flag flying yet.

The Tyrant sometimes waxeth strong
   To drag a fate more fearful down :
He veileth Justice who ere long
   Shall see Eternal Justice frown.
The Kings of Crime from near and far
   Shall come to crown him with their crown
Under the shadow of doom his Star
   Will redden, and go down.

And day shall dawn when it hath set,
But, keep the Old Flag flying yet.

Leaves fall, but lo! the young buds peep!
    Flowers die and still their seed shall bloom;
From death the quick young life will leap
    When Spring goes by the wintry tomb.
And tho' their graves are lusht, in stern
    Heroic dream the dead men lie!
To God their still white faces turn:
    The murdered do not die.
Will God the Martyrs' seed forget?
No.   Keep the Old Flag flying yet.

This triumph of the spoken word
    Is well, my England, but give heed!
The world leans on thee as a Sword
    For Freedom in her battle-need.
Star of a thousand battles red,
    Be thou the Beacon of the Free!
Turn round thy luminous side, and shed
    God's light o'er land and sea.
Thro' floods, or flames, or bloody sweat,
Keep thou the Old Flag flying yet.

The splendid shiver of brave blood
    . Is thrilling through our England now!

She who so often hath withstood
   The Tyrants, lifts her brightened brow.
God's precious charge we proudly keep
   In circling arms of victory;
With Freedom we shall live, or sleep
   With our dear dead who are free.
God forget us when we forget
To keep the Old Flag flying yet.

1858.

NELSON.

AN OLD MAN-O'-WAR'S-MAN YARN.

Ay, ay, good neighbours, I have seen
  Him! sure as God's my life;
One of his chosen crew I've been;
  Haven't I, old good wife?
God bless your dear eyes! didn't you vow
  To marry me any weather,
If I came back with limbs enow
  To keep my soul together.

Brave as a lion was our Nel,
  And gentle as a lamb:
'Tell you it warms my blood to tell
  The tale—grey as I am—
It makes the old life in me climb,
  It sets my soul a-swim;
I live twice over every time
  That I can talk of him.

Our best beloved of all the brave
  That ever for freedom fought;

And all his wonders of the wave
  For fatherland were wrought !
He was the manner of man to show
  How victories may be won ;
So swift, you scarcely saw the blow ;
  You lookt—the deed was done.

You should have seen him as he trod
  The deck, our joy, and pride !
You should have seen him, like a god
  Of storm, his war-horse ride !
You should have seen him as he stood
  Fighting for his good land,
With all the iron of soul and blood
  Turned to a sword in hand.

He sailed his ships for work ; he bore
  His sword for battle-wear ;
His creed was " Best man to the fore !"
  And he was always there.
Up any peak of peril where
  There was but room for one :
The only thing he did not dare
  Was any death to shun.

The Nelson touch his men he taught,
  And his great stride to keep ;

His faithful fellows round him fought
  Ten thousand heroes deep.
With a red pride of life, and hot
  For him, their blood ran free ;
They "minded not the showers of shot,
  No more than peas," said he.

Napoleon saw our sea-king thwart
  His landing on our isle ;
He gnashed his teeth, he gnawed his heart,
  At Nelson of the Nile,
Who set his fleet in flames, to light
  The lion to his prey,
And lead Destruction through the night
  Upon his dreadful way.

Around the world he drove his game,
  And ran his glorious race ;
Nor rested till he hunted them
  From off the ocean's face ;
Like that old war-dog who, till death,
  Clung to the vessel's side
Till hands were lopped, and then with teeth
  He held on till he died.

Oh, he could do the deeds that set
  Old fighters' hearts a-fire ;

The edge of every spirit whet,
  And every arm inspire.
Yet I have seen upon his face
  The tears that, as they roll,
Show what a light of saintly grace
  May clothe a sailor's soul.

And when our darling went to meet
  Trafalgar's Judgment-day,
The people knelt down in the street
  To bless him on his way.
He felt the country of his love
  Watching him from afar;
It saw him through the battle move:
  His heaven was in that star.

Magnificently glorious sight
  It was in that great dawn!
Like one vast sapphire flashing light,
  The sea, just breathing, shone.
Their ships, fresh painted, stood up tall
  And stately: ours were grim
And weatherworn, but one and all
  In rare good fighting trim.

Our spirits all were flying light,
  And into battle sped,

Straining for it on wings of might,
  With feet of springy tread;
The battle light on every face;
  Its fire in every eye;
Our sailor blood at swiftest pace
  To catch the victory nigh.

His proudly-wasted face, wave-worn,
  Was loftily serene;
I felt the brave, bright spirit burn
  There, all too plainly seen;
As though the sword this time was drawn
  For ever from the sheath;
And when its work to-day was done,
  All would be dark in death.

His deep eyes glowed like lamps of night,
  Set in the porch of power;
The deed unborn was kindled bright
  Within them at that hour!
The purpose, welded at white heat,
  Cried like some visible Fate,
" To-day, we must not merely beat:
  We must annihilate."

He smiled to see the Frenchman show
  His reckoning for retreat,

With Cadiz port on his lee-bow ;
  And held him then half-beat.
They showed no colours, till we drew
  Them out to strike with there !
Old Victory, for a prize or two,
  Had flags enough to spare.

Mast-high the famous signal ran ;
  Breathless we caught each word :
" England expects that every man
  Will do his duty."   Lord,
You should have seen our faces ! heard
  Us cheering, row on row ;
Like men before some furnace stirred
  To a fiery fearful glow !

Good Collingwood our lee-line led,
  And cut their centre through.
" See how he goes in !" Nelson said,
  As his first broadside flew,
And near four hundred foemen fell.
  Up went another cheer.
" Ah, what would Nelson give," said Coll,
  " But to be with us here ! "

We grimly kept our vanward path ;
  Over us hummed their shot ;

But, silently, we reined our wrath,
    Held on, and answered not,
Till we could grip them face to face,
    And pound them for our own,
Or hug them in a war embrace,
    Till they or we went down.

How calm he was! when first he felt
    The sharp edge of that fight.
Cabined with God alone he knelt;
    The prayer still lay in light
Upon his face, that used to shine
    In battle—flash with life,
As though the glorious blood ran wine,
    Dancing with that wild strife.

" Fight for us, thou Almighty One!
    Give victory once again!
And if I fall, Thy will be done.
    Amen, Amen, Amen!"
With such a voice he bade good-by;
    The mournfullest old smile wore:
" Farewell! God bless you, Blackwood, I
    Shall never see you more."

And four hours after, he had done
    With winds and troubled foam.

The Reaper was borne dead upon
   Our load of harvest home.
Not till he knew the old flag flew
   Alone on all the deep;
Then said he, " Hardy, is that you ?
   Kiss me."   And fell asleep.

Well, 'twas his chosen death below
   The deck in triumph trod ;
'Tis well.   A sailor's soul should go
   From his good ship to God.
He would have chosen death aboard,
   From all the crowns of rest ;
And burial with the patriot sword
   Upon the victor's breast.

" Not a great sinner."   No, dear heart,
   God grant in our death-pain,
We may have played as well our part,
   And feel as free from stain.
We see the spots on such a star,
   Because it burned so bright;
But on the side next God they are
   All lost in greater light.

And so he went upon his way,
   A higher deck to walk,

Or sit in some eternal day,
 And of the old time talk
With sailors old, who, on that coast,
 Welcome the homeward bound;
Where many a gallant soul we've lost,
 And Franklin will be found.

Where amidst London's roar and moil
 That cross of peace upstands,
Like martyr with his heavenward smile,
 And flame-lit, lifted hands,
There lies the dark and mouldered dust;
 But that magnanimous
And mighty seaman's soul, I trust,
 Is living yet with us.

ENGLAND AND LOUIS NAPOLEON.

MAY 1859.

MAJESTIC Mother! Thine was not a brow
To bend, and blindly take a tinsel Crown
From hands like His. Thy glorious Sons have won
More crowns than thou canst wear, tho' all the year
A fresh one glistened daily. These are crowns
Untarnishable by the breath of scorn!
And crowns that never can be melted down
And minted for the market. Thine was not
A soul to wear the fetters that made fast
His stolen throne to him, and gracefully
To drape the imperial purple round, and hide
The blood that splasht there, red till Judgment Day.
He stole on France, deflowered her in the night,
Then tore her tongue out lest she told the tale:
And Statesmen called him friend, and proudly held
Our Banner over him, while moneyed worldlings,
So pleased they knew not on which leg to stand,
Went on their knees, and worshipt his success;
So prostrate in their souls, so prone in dust,
They saw not how the feet were only clay,

For all the golden Image ;—they forgot
How meanest reptiles crawl up tallest towers.

Our England is long-suffering, and slow
Of judgment, lulled by seeming to the last.
And they are busy dreaming their dark dreams,
While she is sleeping sound in trustful peace.
'Tis well for thee, my Country, when the day
Breaks, thou canst never match them in the dark!
Thine eyes are blind where Birds of night see best.
But instinct, that Veiled Prophet of the Soul,
Flashes up, startled from its seeing trance,
As though God's hand had toucht it while we slept.
There's some invisible danger drawing near,
That hath not taken shape yet, but it comes.
The still small voice cries Wake, my Country, wake,
And sleep no more while that Man's in the world.
The treacherous dealer will deal treacherously ;
The lawless Power is still above all Law!
The Foe that cometh at the dead of night
May find the Goodman slumbering with the arms
Too rusted on the walls. Make the Sword sharp!
Watch warily, you lookers from the hill!
Arm every rampart, rock, and tower of Right,
And arm the people : thus securely armed,
We may sit safe and hold the hands of War
In ours, he cannot strike us for the time.

Once more the war-wave surges gaily out
From Paris with its gallant armaments,
In music's pomp, and bannered pride, and dance
Of life light-hearted, and light-headed crests.
The Ghost of Buonaparte hath broken loose
From hell this time ! ripe Scholar in its lore !
With Ruin's lighted torch half hidden in
The Devil's own dark lanthorn.   We shall see
The night-side of Napoleon, as he tracks
His old earth foot-prints black with rusted blood.

Alas! poor Italy ! the Storm of War
From its fire-mountain throne sweeps burning down,
Its purple lava-mantle trails behind,
Embracing all and blasting all its folds.
A sea of soldiery breaks over her ;
Her fair face darkens in the shadow of Swords ;
Destruction drives his ploughshare thro' her soil,
But will he turn her old lost Jewel to light ?
Another crop of young heroic life
Is ready for the Reaper ; it springs fast
In such a land, so watered, with such blood.

Poor fools ! this Despot turned Deliverer is
A sneaking Cutpurse, not a Cutthroat grand,
Like him that lifted up a Sword of fire,
Whose flashes frightened nations ; and went forth

A prairie-flame consuming men as grass :
How dazzlingly his beacon-star, that danced
From crown to crown, did shine above the lands
He covered with his purple and his pall!
He stormed the dizziest heights, and there he
    stood
In sanguine glory! Like a Battle-God
Ruling the strife with face of marble-calm!
The eyes of Heaven that look down on us with
The earnestness of all eternity,
Saw our old world turn blood-red mirroring Him!
Napoleon dilated till he filled
The vision of France instead of Liberty.
And such the glamour of his grandeur, She
Knew not which Image crowned the Column lifted
A heaven above her, in her love and worship.
But this Man leads her eyeless, blind in blood.
He bears a Burglar's Bludgeon, not a Sword :
Great Oath-breaker, and not World-Victor He.

How far the tide may flood, how quick return
With wreck and ruin for its freightage home,
We know not, nor how soon the nether pit
May open and stern Nemesis rise up
For vengeance infinitely terrible!
As in the grim Norse dream Loke lyeth bound
Down at the heart o' the world, so Tyranny keeps

A potent spirit fettered underground,
And o'er it hangs a Serpent horrible
With eyes thro' which all hell crowds up to see
The poison-fire spit in that Spirit's face;
In straining waves it writhes along to squeeze
Its soul of venom into every drop:
And there sits Wife-like Patience at the side,
Catching the poison till her cup will hold
No more, and she must empty it.
Ah, then the poison burns! with one heart-heave
That Spirit's bonds are burst! an Earthquake's born!
It is the Regnarok of Tyranny!

These Despots do but throw with loaded dice;
They lose or win with other will than theirs!
A Goddess blind leads worshippers as blind.
Henceforth we have no part in this man's lot,
No faith in him; he goes his way, we ours:
If we were true to him we must be false
To all our dearest deeds and noblest dreams!
We are no close-chained Mob for one to walk
Over our heads, and kiss the feet that tread!
Our welding oneness binds up all our wounds,
And one heart and one breath make healing life.
We trust in God, and mean to hold our own.
We are not stainless; there are wrongs on wrongs
Crying for Right! the patient heavens have lookt

On many a failing sadly!   England's Star
Hath winkt on many a crime, and thro' the gloom
Suffering still doggeth Sin, to strike at last.
May God forgive us, we are apt to grow
Unmindful of our blessings, and forget
That this is England, and forget how He
Hath wrought for England; that the sacred Ark
Rests on this Ararat; we dare not face
The world with that same faith we dare profess
Kneeling to God.   And so at times we need
A hint from Heaven, and these are often stern.
We tamper with God's silence till He speaks.
May He forsake not England, but in need
Look smilingly upon her!
                    We at least
Will never run beside this Tyrant's car
Of triumph, glorying in the dust we raise!
Our voice shall cry continually his fall,
Tho' but a lonely trumpet in the night,
And spare not him who plots against our land.

O statesmen, ye who lead this noble land,
May you prove wise and worthy! Great good Men,
With hearts that beat to high heroic measures,
And strength still equal to the sternest time;
With faith to fight and patience to work on,
Still knowing these live longer than a Lie!

The pyramid of our power is not complete
Until it touches heaven for its crown !
And if the Bloody Star should turn this way
Its red eye of destruction, fierce to see
The pride and prowess of our might go down
With England for funereal pyre ; then give
No quarter to the foes that strike at us!
Thro' fire and foam flash on them, and strike home !
Like lightnings of the Lord ! fuel the flames
Of Battle with the Revolution's wrecks
That drift upon our shores.   In Tyrant-land
A young Deliverer lies a-dream, and sees
Such splendours in his visions only eyes
When veiled can look on! tell him the time 's come !
He will arise and stretch his hand and snatch
The Sword.   It will be resurrection day !
The Tyrant's fortresses and palaces
Built with the Headsman's scaffold will dissolve ;
The piles of ghastly, gory heads shall turn
To flaming-sworded Spirits ! the dry bones
Will stir and rise up in a dance of life.

You lovers of our England, do but look
On this dear country over whose fair face
God droopt a bridal veil of tender mist,
That she might keep her beauty virginal,
And he might see her thro' a softer glory :

So very meek and reverent doth she stand
Within this shadow soft of Love Divine,
More loveable, and not as brighter lands
Whose bolder beauty stares up in heaven's face.
Look on her now, this jewel of the world,
Set in that marriage-ring of circling sea !
She smiles upon her Image in its calm,
Like some proud Ship that floateth in its shadow.
And as a happy lover clasps his Bride,
The fond Sea folds her round, and his brimmed life
Runs rippling to her inmost heart of hearts,
Until it swims a-flood with happiness ;
And all the waters of her love leap back
To him exultant from a thousand hills.
From his salt virtue comes her northern sweetness.
How his rough kisses make her roses bloom !
Once in his rouséd wrath he lifted up
A mighty Armada in his arms, and dasht
It into sea-drift at his Mistress' feet.
And still he threatens with his voice of storms
The plots of all Invaders ; still he keeps
Eternal watch around.   How proud in peace,
The wild white horses rear and foam along
And bring to her the harvests of the world !
How grand in war they bear her battle line
In strength half-smiling, perfect Power crowned
With careless grace, which seemeth to all eyes

The plume of Triumph nodding as it goes ;
For visible victory sits upon her brow,
And shines upon her sails.

              See where she sits
Holding at heart her noble dead, and nursing
Her living Children on the old brave virtue !
Wearing the rainy radiance of the morning,
With silver sweetness swimming in her tears,
Feeling the glory rippling down from heaven
With smiles from all her wild flowers, her green leaves,
And nooks where old times live their shepherd ways.
We cannot count her heroes who lay down
In quiet graveyards when their work was done ;
But mound on mound they rise all over the land
To bar a Tyrant's path, and make his feet
To stumble like the blind man among tombs.
Her brave dead make our earth heroic dust :
Their spirit glitters in our England's face
And makes her shine, a Star in blackest night,
Calm at her heart, and glory round her head.
We think of all who fought, and who are now
Immortals in the heaven of her love ;
The Martyrs who have made of burning wrongs
Their fiery chariot, and gone up to God ;
The saintly Sorrows that now walk in white ;
Till faces bloom like battle Banners flusht
All over with most glorious memories.

We are a chosen People ; Freedom wears
Our English Rose for her peculiar crest,
Whoso dare touch it bleeds upon the thorn :
It may be that the time will come again
For one more desperate struggle to the death.
The Devil's eye upon our England looks
With snaky sparkle still. It may be they
Will rouse the tamed Berserkir rage, and make
The vein of wrath throb livid on her brow,
And wake the old Norse War-dog in her blood,
Until she springs afloat upon the sea
Like an Immortal white-winged on the air,
The joy of swiftness lightning thro' her veins.

Thrice hath our England swept the seas, and cleared
Her ocean path, the highways of the world,
And shall again if Robbers lie in wait.
She hath stood fast when towering nations poured
In one wild wave their culminating power !
Thro' all that harvest-day of bloody death,
They charged in vain, and dasht upon the edge
Of her good sword, and fell, at Waterloo !
We kept the shamble slopes of Inkermann !
Thro' blood and fire and gloom of Indian War
We swam the Red Sea, and rode out the storm !
So shall we hold our own dear land with all
The old unvanquisht soul, and we shall see

Their changing Empires shift like sand around
The Island Rock, the footstool of the Lord,
Where Freedom also lays her head, and rest
In calm or storm the best hopes of a world.

Ah, let the Peacemen preach, but let our Peace
Be Right victorious, not triumphant Wrong!
Peace in her white robes, not white-livered Peace!
These pallid Peacemen are to true men what
Our world might be without its iron ore;
But never may the grand old bravery die.
No, no! we must not let the death-fires dance
Along our heights with their funereal flames,
As Hell had thrust up many red-hot tongues
To get its lap of blood when earth is drencht.
Our green fields must not blush in blood for us!
We must not let them pluck the old land down
To throne them in her seat; they must not wear
The Crown she raced for round the world and won.
Our country has a name and fame might fill
The eyes of Hate and Envy with tame tears;
And they shall never lay her low while we
Are true to her in heart and head and hand.
And all who come in peace will find a home,
And all who come in war a mouthful of
Our dust in death, and Sea-beach for a grave.

Great starry thoughts grow luminous in the dark!
The Bird of Hope goes singing overhead!
We cannot fear for England, we can die
To do her bidding, but we cannot fear;
We who have heard her thunder-roll of deeds
Reverberating thro' the centuries;
By battle fire-light had the stories told;
We who have seen how proudly she prepares
For sacrifice, how radiantly her face
Flasht when the Bugle blew its bloody sounds,
And bloody weather fluttered her old Flag;
We who have seen her with the red heaps round!
We who have known the mightiest powers dasht
    back
Broken from her impregnable sea-walls;
We who have learned how in the darkest hour
The greatest light breaks out, and in the time
Of trial she reveals her noblest strength;
For we have felt her big heart beat in ours.

Hail to thee, Mother of Nations! mighty yet
To strive and suffer, and give overthrow!
For all the powers of nature fight for thee.
Spirits that sleep in glory shall awake,
Come down and drive thy Car of victory
Over thine enemies' necks.

      Long will they wait
Who privily lurk to stab thee when the night
Shall cover all in darkness.
        Dear old Land,
Thy shining glories are no Sunset gleams,
But clouds that kindle round some great new Dawn.

THE SEA-KINGS.

THE Spaniard thought to wear our crown,
   Three hundred years ago ;
And bend the head of England down
   To kiss the Pope's great toe !
And next the Dutchman swept the sea
   With besom top-mast high.
Gone is their ocean sovereignty ;
   To-day, how low they lie !

And now the Frenchman's old wounds burn,
   Like devils in their pain ;
They bode the weather of war will turn
   To a bath of bloody rain.
Tingle and ring the ears of France,
   With sounds of battle hymns ;
As on Ambition's dark, mad trance
   The bloody vision swims.

Sons of the old Norse Sailors brave,
   We fill their place to-day ;
No wreath of foam upon the wave,
   To flash and pass away :

Our perilous prize we guard and keep,
   Till last relief God brings;
Then lie in calm majestic sleep,
   Along with the old Sea-Kings.

Well may your proud eyes sparkle, ye
   Rough Sea-Kings young and old;
The salt sea-spirit laughs to see
   The Frenchman grown so bold!
Sword-bayonets, rifled cannon may
   The poor of heart alarm;
But pluck at last must win the day,
   With naked strength of arm.

We are not beaten at a dash;
   Not swiftly overthrown;
Let ship with ship together lash,
   We know who must go down.
No man in Gallic land will live
   To see us dispossessed;
When our Sun sets at sea, we give
   Our Glory to the West.

Those old unconquerable waves,
   They mock at Tyranny;
And never can a land of slaves
   Be Ruler of the Sea.

But would you know their Empress, now
  Behold her! where she smiles;
This diadem on Ocean's brow;
  His Glory of the Isles.

We've fed the Sea with English souls;
  And every mounded wave
To heaven bears witness, for it rolls
  Some English seaman's grave.
Our rivers bear heroic dust
  For burial in that sea,
Which helps to keep our noble trust,
  And battles for the free.

We cannot always down the path
  Of peace and dalliance tread;
Ofttimes the Chosen people hath
  To climb with footprints red:
Our highest life with cross, and scorn,
  And tears, may yet be trod;
And England wear her crown of thorn,
  Whose Roses bloom in blood.

We have immortal quarrel with
  The men who war with Right:
We will not own him, kin or kith,
  Who fails us in this fight!

No room for him on English ground ;
　No bed in Ocean's breast,
Who draws her purple curtains round
　Unfathomable rest.

If those old Greeks for Beauty wrought
　Their ten-years' daring deed,
Shall it be said that less we fought,
　For Freedom in her need ?
No ! Fight till all the Brave lie dead,
　And grass grows on the mart ;
But Freedom here shall rest her head,
　Upon old England's heart.

Like some old Eagle on her nest,
　Up in her own high place,
Our England sits with brooding breast,
　And looks with sharpened face ;
She feels the Shadow of a Hand,
　But, ere it touch her brood,
The Sea, that narrows round our land,
　Shall be a Moat of blood.

Wave out, Old Bird ! or still brood on !
　They shall not bring you low ;
A thousand years have come and gone,
　A thousand more shall go,

Our True Hearts still shall tread the deck;
　Our Ships sail every Sea;
And ride like those who rein the neck
　Of rearing Tyranny.

We've mounted many a windy wave;
　We've weathered many storms;
Unshaken still can hear them rave,
　Safe in the eternal arms !
For, if the worst comes, every man
　We'll perish in our place;
And then the Frenchman—if he can—
　May lead the New Sea Race.

ROBIN BURNS.

I.

A HUNDRED years ago this morn,
    He came to walk our human way;
And we would change the Crown of Thorn
    For healing leaves To-day.

But we can only hang our wreath
    Upon the cold white marble's brow;
Tho' loud we speak, or low we breathe,
    We cannot reach him now.

He loved us all! he loved so much!
    His heart of love the world could hold;
And now the whole wide world, with such
    A love, would round him fold.

'Tis long and late before it wakes
    So kindly,—yet a true world still;
It hath a heart so large, it takes
    A Century to fill.

II.

Aye, tell the wondrous tale to-day,
    When songs are sung, and warm words said ;
Tell how he wore the hodden gray,
      And won the oaten bread.

With wintry welcome at the door,
    Did Nature greet him to his lot ;
Our royal Minstrel of the Poor
      Hid in an old clay Cot.

There in the bonny Bairn-time dawn,
    He nestled at his Mother's knee,
With such a face as might have drawn
      The Angels down to see

A rosy Innocent at prayer,—
    So pure and ready for the hand
Of Her who is Guardian Spirit where
      Babes sleep in Silent Land.

There young Love slily came to bring
    Rare balms that will bewitch the blood
To dance, while happy spirits sing,
      With life in hey-day flood :

And there she found her darling Child,
  The robust Muse of sun-browned health,
Who nurst him up into the wild
   Young heir of all her wealth.

And there she rockt his infant thought
  Asleep with visions glorious,
That hallow now the Poor Man's Cot
   For evermore to us.

Disguised Angelic playmates are
  Those still ideal dreams of Youth,
That draw it on to Greatness; there
   We find them shaped in truth.

Yes, there he learned the touch that thrills
  Right to the natural heart of things;
Struck rootage down to where Life heals
   At the eternal springs.

Before the lords of earth there stood
  A Man by Nature born and bred,
To show us on what simple food
   A hero may be fed.

No gifts of gold for him ; no crown
　　Of Fortune waiting for his brow !
But wrestling strength to earn his own :
　　It shines in glory now !

III.

Wild music on lone shingly shores,—
　　Wild winds that break in seas of sound ;
Sad gloamings eerie on the moors ;
　　The murdered Martyr's mound ;

Wan awful Shadows, trailing like
　　The great skirts of the hurrying Storm ;
Bronzed purple thunder-lights that strike
　　The woodlands wet and warm ;

Meek glimpses of peculiar grace,
　　Where Beauty lyeth, in undress,
Asleep in secret hiding place,
　　Out in the wilderness :

Those glorious Sunsets, God's good-night,
    Is smiled thro' to our world, and felt ;
All, all enrich his ear and sight,—
    Thro' all his being melt.

He rose up in a dawn of light
    That burst upon the olden day ;
Many weird voices of the night
    In his music passed away !

He caught them, Witch and Warlock, ere
    They vanisht ; all the revelry
Of wizard wonder, we must wear
    The mask of Sleep to see !

Droll Humours came for him to paint
    Their pictures ; straight his merry eye
Had taken them, so queer and quaint,
    We laugh until we cry.

K

IV.

He knew the sorrows of poor folk,
    He felt for all their patient pain;
And from his clouded soul he shook
    A music soft as rain.

For them his eyes would brim with balm,
    Dark eyes, and flashing as the levin—
Grew at a touch as sweet and calm
    As are the eyes of Heaven.

So rich in sadness is his breast
    That tenderness, heaven-mirroring, fills;
As lies the soft blue lake at rest
    Among the rugged Hills.

And quick as Mother's milk will rise
    At thrill of her Babe's touch, and strong;
It heaves his heart; it floods his eyes;
    It overflows his song.

But none dare sneer, who see the tear
 In Robin Burns' honest eye;
With all the weakness, it comes clear
  From where the Thunders lie!

Such Ardours flash from out that dew,
 And quiver in that pearl of pain;
As thrills the Spirit of Lightning thro'
 A drop of tempest rain.

In Life's low ways and starless night,
 The Poor so often have to creep
Where Manhood may not walk full height,
 And this made Robin weep.

V.

Of all the Birds the Robin he
 Is darling of the gentle poor;
His nest is sacred; he goes free
  By window or by door;

His lot is lowly, and his wings
 Are only of the homely brown ;
But in the rainy day he sings,
 When gayer friends have flown ;

And hoarded up for us he brings
 In that brave breast of bonny red,
A gathered glory of the springs
 And summers long long fled:

Even so, all Birds of Song above,
 To which the poor man smiling turns,
The darling of his listening love
 Is gentle Robin Burns.

His summer soul our winter warms ;
 He makes a glory in our gloom ;
His nest is safe from all the storms
 For ever in our home.

Yes, there is such a human glow
 Of life and love in Robin's breast;
Its warmth can melt the winter snow
 In Poverty's cold nest.

VI.

His ministers of Music win
  Their way where night is all so mirk,
You scarce can see the Devil in
  That darkness at his work !

Or feel the face of friend from foes :
  But these song-spirits softly come ;
And lo ! a light of heaven glows
  Within the meanest home :

On either side the hearth they glide,
  And take the empty seat of Care ;
Immortal Presences that bide
  In blessed beauty there.

They set us singing at our work,
  And where no easing voice is found,
Out smiles the music that may lurk
  In thoughts too fine for sound.

They weave some pictured tints that shine
　　Luminous in life's cold grey woof;
They make the vine of Patience twine
　　About the barest roof.

More sweet his songs to him who plods
　　Shut up in smoky city prison,
Than to the cagèd Lark cool sods
　　Cut ere the sun be risen.

The Soldier feels them as a spring
　　Of healing, mid the Indian sand :
They gush from out his heart; they bring
　　Such news of the Old Land.

Ah, how some old sweet cradle song
　　The wayward wandering soul still brings
Home! Home again; with ties as strong
　　As Love's own leading-strings.

We hug the Homestead, and more near
　　The fresh and fonder tendrils twine,
To make our clasp more close, for fear
　　Our dear ones we may tine.

VII.

When Hesper, thro' some shady nook,
    Sparkles on Lovers face to face,
Where droopt lids shade a burning look
      With Beauty's shyer grace—

And holy is the hour for love;
    And all so silent comes the Night,
Lest even a breath of faëric move
      That poise so feather light—

Where two hearts weigh, to blight or bless,
    Till swarming like a summer hive,
The inner world of happiness
      With music grows alive—

There, as Life aches so, heart in heart,
    And hand in hand so fondly yearns,
Love shakes his wings, and soars and sings
      Some song of Robin Burns.

VIII.

Think how those Heroes, true till death,
    In Lucknow listened thro' the strife,
And held, what seemed their latest breath
    They had to draw in life,

To hear the old Scots' music dear
    Ask, down the battle pauses brief,
As Havelock's men with fire and cheer
    Swept in to their relief—

" Should auld acquaintance be forgot ? "
    Thro' flaming hell we come ! we come !
To keep that pledge, not given for nought,
    Around the hearth at home !

" We'll take a cup of kindness " here,
    For Scotland yet, and Auld Lang Syne ;
Aye, tho' that cup be filled with dear
    Heart's blood instead of wine !

' And here's a hand my trusty fere ; "
　　And then it seemed the dear old Land
Did burst their tomb, the death-shroud tear,
　　And clasp them with her hand.

IX.

How dearly Robin lo'ed the land
　　That gave such gallant heroes birth ;
Its wee blue bit of heaven, and
　　Its dear green nook of earth !

And dearer is the purple heath ;
　　The bonny broom of beamless gold ;
And sweeter is the mellow breath
　　Of Autumn on the wold ;

Where he once lookt with glorious gaze,
　　In all our way-side wanderings,
Shy Beauty lifts her veil of haze,
　　And smiles in common things :

The Daisy opes its eye at dawn,
    And straight from Nature's heart so true,
The tear of Burns peeps sparkling! an
    Immortal drop of dew!

With eyes a thought more tender we
    Look on all dumb and helpless things;
In his large love they stand, as he
    Had sheltered them with wings.

Down by the singing burn we greet
    His voice of love and liberty;
High on the bleak hill side we meet
    His spirit blithe and free:

And on this land should Foe e'er tread,
    He will fight for it at our side;
Flame on our banners overhead;
    In songs of victory ride.

X.

A Hundred years ago To-day,
    This great and glorious Stranger came;
Men wondered as he went his way,
    A wild and wandering flame!

The fiercer fire of life confined,
    With higher wave 'twill heave and break;
And higher should the mountain mind
    Thrust up a starward peak!

But often is the kindling clay
    With its red lightnings rent and riven;
And Earth holds up a wreck to pray
    For the healing hand of Heaven.

Round such a soul more sternly warred
    The powers that smite for Wrong and Right;
Till thunder-scathed, and battle-scarred,
    Death bore him from the fight.

But now we recognize in him
        One of the high and shining race;
All gone the mortal mists that dim
        The fair immortal face!

The splendour of a thousand suns
        Is shining; and the tearful rain
No more with passionate pathos runs;
        And there is no more pain.

The sorrow and suffering, soil of shame,
        All gone; all far away have passed;
He sitteth in the heaven of fame,
        Quietly crowned at last.

The prowling Ghoul hath left his grave;
        Husht is the praying Pharisee;
His frailties fade, his virtues brave
        Live, work immortally.

XI.

Weep, weep, exulting tears that He,
 The lowly born, the Peasant's son,
Hath wrought for us imperishably ;
 A peerless place hath won !

And such a Crown to bind thy brow,
 Thy glorious Child hath gained for thee,
Thou grey old nurse of Heroes !   Thou
 Proud Mother, Poverty !

Look up ! and let the big tears be
 Triumphant, toucht with sparks of pride ;
Look up ! in His great glory we
 Are also glorified.

Or weep the tear that Pity wrings,
 To think his brightness he should dim ;
Then 'tis the tear of sorrow brings
 Us nearer unto him.

'Tis here we touch his garment; here
    The poorest, or the frailest, earns
The right to call him kinsman dear;
    Our Brother, Robin Burns.

In fires of suffering far more fair
    We forge the precious bond of love:
Ah! Robin, if God hear our prayer,
    'Tis all made well above.

And you, who comforted His Poor
    In this world, have eternal home
With those He comforteth, His Poor,
    Thro' all the world to come.

Your Highland Mary went before,
    To plead for you in saintly sooth,
Whom she remembered when you wore
    The pureness of your youth!

With those great Bards who live for aye,
    Your faults and failings all forgiven,
May there be festival to-day,
    And a great joy in heaven.

The truth, afar off, found at last ;
    The triumph rung impetuously,
Thro' all that Crystal Palace vast
    Of white Eternity.

XII.

Dear Robin, could you but return
    Once more, how changed it all would be ;
The heart of this wide world doth yearn
    To take you welcomingly.

Warm eyes would shine at windows ; quick
    Warm hands would clasp you at the door,
Where oft they let you pass heart-sick,
    So heedlessly of yore.

And they would have you wear the Crown,
    Who bade you bear the crushing cross ;
Their glorious gain was all unknown
    Without the bitter loss.

The cup you carried was so filled;
　　The pressing crowd, so eager round,
Dragged down your lifted arm, and spilled
　　　　Such dear drops on the ground!

How we would comfort your distress;
　　Would see you smile as once you smiled;
And hold your hands in silentness;
　　　　Strong Man and little Child!

Your poor heart heaving like the waves
　　Of seas that moan for evermore,
And try to creep into the caves
　　　　Of Rest, but find no shore,—

Poor heart, come rest thee from the strife;
　　Come rest thee, rest thee in the calm,
We'd cry; come bathe thy weary life
　　　　In Love's immortal balm.

XIII.

We cannot see your face, Robin !
    Your flashing lip, your fearless brow :
We cannot hear your voice, Robin !
    But you are with us now.

Altho' the mortal face is dark
    Behind the veil of spirit-wings ;
You draw us up as Heaven the Lark,
    When its music in him sings.

With tender awe we feel you near ;
    You make our lifted faces shine ;
You brim our cup with kindness here,
    For sake of Auld Lang Syne.

We are one at heart as Britain's Sons,
    Because you join our clasping hands ;
While one electric feeling runs
    Thro' all the English lands.

And near or far, where Britons band
    To-day, the leal and true heart turns
More fondly to the fatherland,
    For love of Robin Burns.

THE FIGHTING TEMERAIRE

TUGGED TO HER LAST BERTH.

It is a glorious tale to tell,
  When nights are long and mirk,
How well she fought our fight; how well
  She did our England's work;
      Our good ship Temeraire;
      The fighting Temeraire!
She goeth to her last long home,
      Our grand old Temeraire.

Bravely over the breezy blue,
  They went to do or die;
And proudly on herself she drew
  The Battle's burning eye!
      Our good ship Temeraire;
      The fighting Temeraire!
She goeth to her last long home,
      Our grand Old Temeraire.

Round her the glory fell in flood,
  From Nelson's loving smile,
When, raked with fire, she ran with blood,
  In England's hour of trial!

Our good ship Temeraire;
The fighting Temeraire!
She goeth to her last long home,
Our grand old Temeraire.

And when our darling of the sea
Sank dying on his deck;
With her revenging thunders, she
Struck down his foe—a Wreck!
Our good ship Temeraire;
The fighting Temeraire!
She goeth to her last long home,
Our grand old Temeraire.

And when our victory stayed the rout,
And Death had stilled the storm,
How gallantly she led them out—
Her prize on either arm!
Our good ship Temeraire;
The fighting Temeraire!
She goeth to her last long home,
Our grand old Temeraire.

Her day now draweth to its close,
With solemn sunset crowned;
To death her crested beauty bows;
The night is folding round,

Our good ship Temeraire;
The fighting Temeraire!
She goeth to her last long home,
Our grand old Temeraire.

No more the big heart in her breast,
Will heave from wave to wave;
Weary and war-worn, ripe for rest,
She glideth to her grave,
Our good ship Temeraire;
The fighting Temeraire!
She goeth to her last long home,
Our grand old Temeraire..

In her dumb pathos desolate
As night among the dead!
Yet wearing an exceeding weight
Of glory on her head.
Our good ship Temeraire;
The fighting Temeraire!
She goeth to her last long home,
Our grand old Temeraire.

Good bye! good bye! Old Temeraire;
A sad, a proud good bye!
The stalwart spirit that did wear
Your sternness, shall not die.

Our good ship Temeraire ;
The fighting Temeraire !
She goeth to her last long home,
Our grand old Temeraire.

Thro' battle blast, and storm of shot,
Your Banner we shall bear ;
And fight for it, like those who fought
Your guns, old Temeraire !
The fighting Temeraire ;
The conquering Temeraire ;
She goeth to her last long home,
Our grand old Temeraire.

RIFLE VOLUNTEERS.

You leal high hearts of England,
  The evil days are near,
When we with steel in heart and hand,
  Must strike for all that's dear.
And better to tread the bloodiest deck,
  Or fieriest field of fame,
Than break the heart, and bow the neck,
  And sit in the shadow of shame.
Let Despot, Death or Devil come,
  United here we stand:
We'll safely guard our Island-Home,
  Or die for the dear old Land.

O Volunteers of England,
  You'll hurry to her call;
And our good Ship shall sail the storm,
  With its merry mariners all.
In words we need not waste our breath,
  But, be the Trumpet blown,

And in the Battle's dance of death,
   We'll dance the bravest down.
Let Despot, Death or Devil come,
   United here we stand ;
We'll safely guard our Island-Home,
   Or die for the dear old Land.

Success to our dear England,
   Should dark days come again ;
And may she rise up glorious
   As the rainbow after rain :
A thousand memories warm us still,
   And, ere the old spirit dies,
The purple of each wold and hill
   From our best blood shall rise.
Let Despot, Death or Devil come,
   United here we stand ;
We'll safely guard our Island-Home,
   Or die for the dear old Land.

God strike with our dear England ;
   And long may the old land be,
The guiding glory of the world ;
   Home of the fair and free !
Old ocean on his silver shield
   Uplifts our little Isle,

Unvanquisht still by flood or field,
　While the heavens in blessing smile.
Let Despot, Death or Devil come,
　United here we stand ;
We'll safely guard our Island-Home,
　Or die for the dear old Land.

NAVAL VOLUNTEERS.

Come, show your colours now, my Lads,
  That all the world may know
The Boys are equal to their Dads,
  Whatever blast may blow.
England, as Mistress of the Sea,
Shall rule in boundless sovereignty.

All Hands aboard ! our country calls
  On her seafaring folk !
In giving up our wooden Walls,
  More need for Hearts of Oak !
England, as Mistress of the Sea,
Shall rule in boundless sovereignty.

Remember how that old Fire-Drake
  Did singe the Spaniard's beard ;
And think how Raleigh, Nelson, Blake,
  Into their harbours steered !
England, as Mistress of the Sea,
Shall rule in boundless sovereignty.

Think how o' nights we cut them out!
   'Twas—many a time and oft—
Silence!—a rush—a tug—a shout!—
   And the old flag flew aloft :
England, as Mistress of the Sea,
Shall rule in boundless sovereignty!

Be it one to seven—hell or heaven !
   We've fought our decks red-wet ;
Be it hell or heaven!—one to seven !
   We fear no foemen yet !
England, as Mistress of the Sea,
Shall rule in boundless sovereignty!

That secret in the Sphinx's eyes
   Must have solution stern ;
There is but one more throw o' the dice,
   And then 'twill be our turn !
England, as Mistress of the Sea,
Shall rule in boundless sovereignty !

At every port-hole there shall flame
   The same fierce battle-face,
All worthy of the old sea fame,
   All of the old sea race !
England, as Mistress of the Sea,
Shall rule in boundless sovereignty !

Alone, aloft in her right hand
　　She bears her flag unfurled ;
One foot on sea and one on land,
　　The bulwark of a world.
England, as Mistress of the Sea,
Shall rule in boundless sovereignty !

OUR NATIVE LAND.

THIS is our Mother Country!
    The dearest Land,
    The rarest Land,
Round which the sea keeps sentry,
    Or Ships are manned;
    Or Ships are manned;
Nothing but Heaven above her!
    And here's my hand,
    And here's my hand.
We are Brothers all who love her!
    Our Native Land,
    Dear Native Land.

Afar and near they hail her
    With greetings warm,
    With greetings warm.
The famous old brave Sailor,
    That rode the storm,
    Aye, many a storm.

Who would not die to save her
    Shall bear the brand,
    The Coward's brand.
Our love must never waver
    For Native Land,—
    Dear Native Land.

No matter where our place is,
    We may go forth,
    We may go forth,
And turn dead frozen faces,
    Home from the North ;
    Home from the North.
Or sink, 'neath Orient heaven,
    In burning sand,
    Waste, desert sand.
Our lives shall still be given
    For Native Land,
    Dear Native Land.

And long may such life nourish
    The old land on,
    This dear land on ;
And long, long may she flourish
    When we are gone,—
    All dead and gone.

Long may the sea caress her,
    As great and grand,
    As great and grand.
Thou GOD in Heaven bless her!
    Our Native Land,
    Dear Native Land.

Ofttimes the foe beheld us,
    All torn apart,
    All torn apart;
Altho' a blow would weld us
    All one at heart,
    All one at heart.
Now trust we in each other,
    A little band,
    A happy band;
The Children of one Mother,
    Our Native Land,
    Dear Native Land!

Some new heroic story
    The world shall learn,
    The world shall learn,
If we who keep her glory
    Are true and stern,
    All true and stern.

Come wild and warring weather,
    We ready stand,
    All ready stand,
To fight or fall together
    For Native Land,
    Dear Native Land!

A NATIONAL ANTHEM.

God bless our native Land,
Glorious, and grave, and grand ;
  God bless our Land !
God bless her noble face ;
God bless her peerless race ;
Great heart, and daring hand,
  God bless our Land.

God love our English Land ;
Make her for ever grand ;
  God love our Land !
Robe her with righteousness ;
Crown her with gifts of grace ;
Throne her at Thy right hand ;
  God love our Land.

If secret foes should band
To strike our dear old Land,
  God aid our Land !

M

Be Thou her strength and stay,
God, in the battle-day!
Strew them ashore like sand;
        God aid our Land.

Few are we, Sword in hand;
All Sword in soul we stand,
        Around our Land!
And when her blood shall flow,
Green make her glory grow,
Lead her in triumph grand,
        Our leal old Land.

Here pray we hand in hand,
Tears in our eyelids stand;
        God save our Land!
Thy Watch-tower on the Sea;
Venger of Right is she;
Long let old Fear-not stand,
        God save our Land!

CHRISTIE'S POEMS.

FOR CHRISTIE'S SAKE.

Upon us falls the shadow of Night,
   And darkened is our day;
My Love will greet the morning light,
   Four hundred miles away;
God love her! borne so swift and far
   From hearts so like to break;
And God love all who are good to her;
     For Christie's sake.

I know whatever spot of ground,
   In any land, we tread—
I know the eternal arms are round;
   That Heaven is overhead;
And faith the mourning heart will heal;
   But many fears will make,
Our spirits faint, our fond hearts kneel,
     For Christie's sake.

Good bye, dear ! be they kind to you,
   As tho' you were their ain ;
My Daisy opens to the dew,
   But shuts against the rain !
Never will New Moon glad our eyes,
   But offerings we shall make,
To old God Wish ! and prayers will rise,
     For Christie's sake.

Four years ago we struck our tent ;
   O'er homeless Babes we yearned ;
Our all—three darlings—with us went,
   But only two returned !
While life yet bleeds into *her* grave,
   Love ventures one more stake ;
Hush ! hush ! poor hearts ! if big, be brave ;
     For Christie's sake.

Like Crown to most ambitious brows,
   Was Christie to us given ;
To make our Home a holy house,
   And nursery of Heaven.
O softer was her bed of rest
   Than lily's on the lake ;
Peace filled so deep each billowy breast,
     For Christie's sake.

To music played by harps and hands
    Invisible, were we drawn
O'er charmed seas, thro' fairy lands,
    Under a dearer dawn ;
We entered our new world of love,
    With blessings in our wake ;
And prospering heavens smiled above,
        For Christie's sake.

We gazed with proud eyes luminous,
    On such a gift of grace ;
All heaven narrowed down to us,
    In one dear little face !
And many a pang we felt, dear Wife,
    With hurt of heart and ache,
All shut within like clasping knife,
        For Christie's sake.

I would no tears might e'er run down
    Her patient face, beside
Such happy pearls of heart as crown
    Young Mother—new-made Bride ;
For 'tis a face that, looking up
    To passing Heaven, might make
An Angel stop ; a blessing drop ;
        For Christie's sake.

If Love in that Child's heart of hers
  Should breathe, and break its calm,
With trouble sweet as that which stirs
  The brooding buds of balm,—
Listening at ear of peeping pearl;
  Glistening in eyes that shake
Their sweet dew down! God bless our Girl!
    For Christie's sake.

But Father! if our Babe must mourn,
  Be merciful and kind;
And if our gentle Lamb be shorn,
  Attemper Thou the wind!
Over the deluge guide our Dove,
  And to thy bosom take
With arm of love and shield above;
    For Christie's sake.

We have had sorrows many and strange.
  Poor Christie! when I'm gone,
Some of my words will wierdly change
  If she read sadly on:
Lightnings, from what was dark of old,
  With meanings strange will break,
Of sorrows hid, or dimly told,
    For Christie's sake.

Wife! we should still try hard to win,
　　The best for our dear child ;
And keep her resting place within,
　　When all without grows wild.
As on the winter graves the snow
　　Falls softly, flake by flake,
Our love should whitely clothe our woe ;
　　　　For Christie's sake.

For one will wake at midnight drear
　　From out a dream of death,
And find no dear head pillowed near ;
　　No sound of peaceful breath ;
May no weak wailing words arise,
　　No bitter thoughts awake,
To see the tears in Memory's eyes ;
　　　　For Christie's sake.

And *There!* where many crownless Kings
　　Of Earth a Crown shall wear ;
The Martyrs who have borne the pangs
　　Their palm at last shall bear !
When, with our Lily pure of sin
　　Our heavenward way we take,
There may we walk with welcome in ;
　　　　For Christie's sake.　　·

HUNT THE SQUIRREL.

It was Atle of Vermeland,
  In winter used to go
A hunting up in the Pine Forest,
  With snow-shoes, sledge, and bow.

Soon his sledge with the soft fine furs
  Was heapt up heavily;
Enough to warm old Winter with;
  And a wealthy man was he.

Just as he was going back home,
  He lookt up into a tree;
There sat a merry brown Squirrel that seemed
  To say—" You can't shoot me!"

And it twinkled all over temptingly,
  To the tip of its tail acurl;
Its humour was arch as the look may be
  Of a would-be-wooed sweet Girl

Who makes the Lover follow her, follow her,
   All his life up-caught!
A-floating on, a-floating on,
   High in the heaven of thought.

Atle he left his sledge and furs!
   All day his arrows rung—
Bun went leaping from bough to bough—
   Only himself they stung.

He hunted far in the deep forest,
   Till died the last day-gleams ;
Then laid him a-weary down to rest
   And hunted it thro' his dreams.

All night long the snow fell fast
   And covered his snug fur-store ;
Long, long did he strain his eyes !
   He found it never more.

Home came Atle of Vermeland ;
   No Squirrel! no furs for the Mart !
Empty head brought empty hand ;
   Both—a very full heart.

Many a one hunts the Squirrel,
   In merry or mournful truth!
Until the gathering snows of age,
   Cover the treasures of Youth.

Deeper into the forest dark,
   The Squirrel will dance all day;
Till eyes grow blind and miss their mark;
   And weary hearts lose their way.

My Darling! should you ever espy,
   This Squirrel up in the tree,
With a dancing Devil in its eye—
   Just let the Squirrel be.

MY MAID MARIAN.

SPRING comes with violet eyes unveiled,
　Her fragrant lips apart!
And Earth smiles up as tho' she held
　Most honeyed thoughts at heart.
But nevermore will Spring arise
Dancing in sparkles of *her* eyes.

A gracious wind low-breathing comes
　As from the fields of God;
The old lost Eden newly blooms
　From out the sunny sod.
My buried joy stirs with the earth,
And tries to sun *its* sweetness forth.

The trees move in their slumbering,
　Dreaming of one that's near!
Put out their feelers for the Spring,
　To wake, and find her here!
My spirit on the threshold stands,
And stretches out its waiting hands.

Then goeth from me in a stream
  Of yearning ; wave on wave
Slides thro' the stillness of a dream,
  To little Marian's grave :
For all the miracle of Spring
My long lost child will never bring.

Where blooms the golden crocus-burst,
  And Winter's tenderling,
There lies our little Snowdrop ! first
  Of Flowers in our love's spring !
How all the year's young beauties blow
About her there, I know, I know.

The Blackbird with his warble wet,
  The Thrush with reedy thrill,
Open their hearts to Spring, and let
  The influence have its will !
Tho' all around the Spring hath smiled,
She seems to have kissed where lies my child.

In purple shadow and golden shine
  Old Arthur's Seat is crowned ;
Like shapes of Silence crystalline
  The great white clouds sail round !
The Dead at rest the long day thro'
Lie calm against the pictured blue.

O Marian, my maid Marian,
　　So strange it seems to me!
That you, the Household's darling one,
　　So soon should cease to be.
Ah, was it that our praying breath
Might kindle heavenward fires of faith?

So much forgiven for your sake
　　When bitter words were said,
And little arms about the neck
　　With blessings bowed the head!
So happy as we might have been,
Our hearts more close with you between.

Dear early Dew-drop! such a gleam
　　Of sun from heaven you drew,
We little thought that smiling beam
　　Would drink our precious dew!
But back to heaven our dew was kissed,
We saw it pass in mournful mist.

Our lowly home was lofty-crowned
　　With three sweet budding girls!
Our sacred marriage-ring set round
　　With darling wee love-pearls!
One jewel from the ring is gone,
One fills a grave in Warriston.

We bore her beauty in our breast,
　　As heaven bears the Dawn,
We brooded over her dear nest,
　　Still close and closer drawn.
Hearts thrilled and listened, watched and throbbed
And strayed not,—yet the nest was robbed!

"Stay yet a little while, Beloved!"
　　In vain our prayerful breath:
Across heaven's lighted window moved
　　The shadow of black Death.
In vain our hands were stretcht to save;
There closed the gateways of the Grave!

Could my death-vision have darkened up
　　In her sweet face, my child;
I scarce should see the bitter cup,
　　I could have drank and smiled:
Blessing her with my last-wrung breath,
Dear Angel in my dream of death.

Her memory is like music we
　　Have heard some singer sing,
That thrills life thro', and echoingly
　　Our hearts for ever ring;
We try it o'er and o'er again,
But ne'er recall that wondrous strain.

My proud heart like a river runs,
　Lying awake o' nights ;
I see her with the shining Ones
　Upon the shining heights.
And a wee Angel-face will peep
Down starlike thro' the veil of sleep.

My yearnings try to get them wings
　And float me up afar,
As in the Dawn the sky-lark springs
　To reach some distant Star
That all night long swam down to him
In brightness, but at morn grew dim.

She is a spirit of light that leavens
　The darkness where we wait ;
And starlike opens in the heavens
　A little golden gate !
O may we wake and find her near
When work and sleep are over here !

No sweetness to this world of ours
　Is without purpose given,
The fragrance that goes up from flowers
　May be their seed in Heaven.
We saw Heaven in her face, may we
Her future face in Heaven see.

In some far spring of brighter bloom,
　　More life, and ampler breath,
My bud hath burst the folding gloom,
　　A-flower from dusty death!
We wonder will she be much grown?
And how will her new name be known?

I saw her ribboned robe this morn,
　　Mine own lost little child;
Wee shoes her tiny feet had worn,
　　And then my heart grew wild.
We only trust our hearts to peep
In on them when we want to weep.

But hearts will break or eyes must weep,
　　And so we bend above
These treasures of old days that keep
　　The fragrance of young love.
The harvest-field tho' reapt and bare
Hath yet a patient gleaner there.

I never think of her sweet eyes
　　In dusky death now dim,
But waters of my heart will rise,
　　And there they smile and swim,
Forget-me-nots so blue, so dear,
Swim in the waters of a tear.

How often in the days gone by
  She lifted her dear head,
And stretcht wee arms for me to lie
  Down in her little bed.
And cradled in my happy breast
Was softly carried into rest.

And now when life is sore oppressed
  And runs with weary wave,
I long to lay me down and rest
  In little Marian's grave;
To smile as peaceful as she smiled—
For I am now the nestling child.

Immortal Love, a spirit of bliss
  And brightness, moves above,
While here forever Sorrow is
  The shadow cast by Love,
But love for her no sorrow will bring
And no more tearful leaves-taking.

No passing sorrows on their march
  Will leave sad foot-prints now,
No troubles strain the tender arch
  Of that white baby brow.
No cares to cloud, no tears that come
To rob the cheek of pearly bloom.

All sweetest shapes that Beauty wears
    Are round about her drawn;
Auroral bloom, and vernal airs,
    And blessings of the dawn;
All loveliness that ne'er grows less;
Time cannot touch her tenderness.

One sparkle of immortal light
    Our love for her shall shine
In the dew-drop that nestles white
    At heart with gleam divine,
But vanishes from Death's cold clasp,
When he the flower of life doth grasp.

The patient calm that comes with years,
    Hath made us cease to fret;
Only at times in sudden tears
    Dumb hearts will quiver yet:
And each one turns the face and tries
To hide WHO looks thro' parent eyes.

CHRISTIE'S POOR OLD GRAN.

No GREEN age, beautiful to see,
    Hath Poor Old Gran :
No ripe life mellowed goldenly,
    Hath Poor Old Gran.
One by one we have left her fold ;
Her lonely hearth is growing cold ;
Faint is her smile as the primrose gold,
    Our Poor Old Gran.

Ah ! whitened face, and withered form
    Of Poor Old Gran !
Beaten and blancht in many a storm :
    Poor Old Gran !
She hath wept the bitter tears that sow
The dark grave-violets in the snow,
Where once the red young rose did glow ;
    Poor Old Gran !

There's few have lived a harder lot ;
    Poor Old Gran !
But she toiled on and murmured not ;
    Poor Old Gran !
For us she toiled on starvingly,
And fought the wolf of poverty ;
Upon her heart's blood suckled me,
    Our Poor Old Gran !

Her river of life hath roughly rolled ;
    Poor Old Gran !
A Wreck lies dark, its tale untold ;
    Poor Old Gran !
Yet shall her old heart laugh with ye,
My Birdsnest in the mouldering tree !
And soft in heaven her bed shall be ;
    Poor Old Gran !

The grip of Poverty is grim ;
    Poor Old Gran !
Lustres of lip and eye soon dim ;
    Poor Old Gran !
But thro' the frailty of her face
There gleams a light of tender grace
Or else I see thro' a tearful haze,
    Poor Old Gran !

You came in all our sorrowings,
     Poor Old Gran!
How your weakness hurried on wings,
     Poor Old Gran!
You stood at Bridal, Birth, and Bier :
Our darlings dead and gone seem near
When you are near, and make more dear
     Our Poor Old Gran!

So come to our Cottage up the lane,
     Poor Old Gran!
Follow our fortune's harvest wain,
     Poor Old Gran!
We'll shelter you from wind and rain,
Hunger you shall not know again,
Plenty shall smile away your pain,
     Poor Old Gran!

And little laughing stars shall rise
     On Poor Old Gran!
In the clear heaven of Childhood's eyes,
     For Poor Old Gran!
Wee fingers, stroking her grey hair,
Shall almost melt the hoarfrost there ;
Wee lips shall kiss away the care
     From Poor Old Gran!

So come and sit beside our hearth,
    Poor Old Gran !
Come from the darkness and the dearth,
    Poor old Gran !
And you shall be our fireside guest,
And weary heart and head shall rest;
And may your last days be your best,
    Poor Old Gran.

THE LEGEND OF LITTLE PEARL.

"Poor little Pearl, good little pearl!"
  Sighed every kindly neighbour;
It was so sad to see a girl
  So tender, doomed to labour.

A wee bird fluttered from its nest
  Too soon, was that meek creature;
Just fit to rest in mother's breast,
  The darling of fond Nature.

God shield poor little ones, where all
  Must help to be bread-bringers!
For once afoot, there's none too small
  To ply their tiny fingers.

Poor Pearl, she had no time to play
  The merry game of childhood ;
From dawn to dark she worked all day,
  A-wooding in the wild wood.

When others played, she stole apart
  In pale and shadowy quiet ;
Too full of care was her child-heart
  For laughter running riot.

Hard lot for such a tender life,
  And miserable guerdon ;
But like a womanly wee wife,
  She bravely bore her burden.

One wintry day they wanted wood
  When need was at the sorest ;
Poor Pearl, without a bit of food,
  Must up and to the forest.

But there she sank down in the snow,
  All over numbed and aching :
Poor little Pearl, she cried as though
  Her very heart was breaking.

The blinding snow shut out the house
    From little Pearl so weary;
The lonesome wind among the boughs
    Moaned with its warnings eerie.

To little Pearl a Child-Christ came,
    With footfall light as fairy;
He took her hand, he called her name,
    The voice was sweet and airy.

His gentle eyes filled tenderly
    With mystical wet brightness:
" And would you like to come with me,
    And wear the robe of whiteness ?"

He bore her bundle to the door,
    Gave her a flower when going:
" My darling, I shall come once more,
    When the little bud is blowing."

Home very wan came little Pearl,
    But on her face strange glory:
They only thought, " What ails the girl ?"
    And laught to hear her story.

Next morning mother sought her child,
And clasped it to her bosom;
Poor little Pearl, in death she smiled,
And the rose was full in blossom.

NEWS OF CHRISTIE.

We read your letters; no word lost;
    All, all is remembered;
And sometimes when there is no post,
    Once more are the old ones read;
Of all she did we love to hear;
    And how the days have sped;
But to our listening hearts most dear
    Is something "Christie said."

FOR EVER.

"Farewell, Sweet! may you find a nest
    Of home in haven dearer;
And happier rest upon the breast
    Of truer love and nearer;
May favours fall, may blessings flow
    For you, may cares come never!
But kiss me, Dear, before you go,
    And then shake hands for ever."

Her very heart within doth melt,
    And gathers, while she lingers,
A weeping warmth, as tho' she felt
    A wee babe's feeling fingers:
The minutes pass; they do not part;
    And vain was all endeavour,
A touch had closed them heart to heart;
    Their hands *were* claspt for ever.

OUR WHITE DOVE.

A WHITE Dove out of heaven flew,
  White as the whitest shape of Grace
  That nestles in the soft embrace
Of heaven when skies are summer blue;

It came with dew-drop purity,
  On glad wings of the morning light;
  And sank into our life, so white
A VISION! sweetly, secretly!

Silently nestled our WHITE DOVE:
  Balmily made our bosoms swim
  With still delight, and overbrim;
The air it breathed was breath of love:

Our Dove had eyes of baby blue,
  Soft as the Speedwell's by the way,
  That looketh up as it would say,
" Who kissed me while I slept, did you?"

God love it! but we took our Bird,
   And loved it well, and merry made ;
   We sang and danced around, or prayed
In silence, wherein hearts are heard.

It seemed to come from far green fields
   To meet us over life's rough sea,
   With leaf of promise from the tree
In which a dearer nest it builds.

As fondling Mother birds will pull
   The softest feathers from their breast,
   We gave our best to line the nest,
And make it warm and beautiful!

We held it as the leaves of life
   In hidden silent service fold
   About a Rose's heart of gold,
So jealous of all outer strife!

When holy sleep in soothing palms
   Pillowed the darling little head,
   How lightly moved we round the bed,
And felt the silence fall in balms!

But all we did or tried to do,
 Our flood of joy it never felt;
 Only into our hearts would melt
Still deeper those dove-eyes of blue.

Quick with the spirit of field and wood,
 All other Birds would sing and sing
 Till hearts did ripple and homes did ring:
Our white Dove only cooed and cooed—

With every day some sweetness new,
 And night and day and day and night
 It was the voice of our delight,
That gentle, low, endearing coo!

God! if we were to lose our child!
 O, we must die, poor hearts would cry:
 She lookt on us so hushingly;
So mournfully to herself she smiled.

One day she pined up in our face
 With a low cry we could not still;
 A moaning we could never heal,
For sleep in some more quiet place.

We could not help, and yet must see
   The little head droop wearily,
   The little eyes shine eerily,
My Dove ! what have they done to thee ?

The look grew pleading in her eyes
   And mournful as the lonesome light
   That in a window burns all night,
Asking for stillness, while one dies.

The hand of Death so coldly clings,
   So strongly draws the weak life-wave
   Into his dark, vast, silent cave ;
Our little Dove must use its wings !

And so it sought the dearer nest ;
   A little way across the sea
   It kept us wingèd company,
Then sank into its loafier rest ;

And left us long ago to feel
   A sadness in the sweetest words ;
   A broken heartstring mid the chords ;
A tone more tremulous when we kneel.

But, dear my Christie, do not cry,
　　Our White Dove left for you and me
　　Such blessed promise as must be
Perfected in the heavens high.

The stars that shone in her dear eyes
　　May be a little while withdrawn,
　　To rise and lead the eternal dawn
For us, up heaven in other skies.

Our Bird of God but soars and sings :
　　Oft when life's heaving wave 's at rest,
　　She makes her mirror in my breast,
I feel a winnowing of wings ;

And meekly doth she minister
　　Glad thoughts of comfort, thrills of pride ;
　　She makes me feel that if I died
This moment I should go to her.

Be good ! and you shall find her where
　　No wind can shake the wee bird's nest ;
　　No dreams can break the wee bird's rest ;
No night, no pain, no parting there !

No echoes of old storms gone by!
   Earth's sorrows slumber peacefully ;
   The weary are at rest, for He
Shall wipe the tears from every eye.

CHRISTIE'S PORTRAIT.

Your tiny Picture makes me yearn ;
    We are so far apart,
My Darling ! I can only turn
    And kiss you in my heart.
A thousand tender thoughts a-wing,
    Swarm in a summer clime,
And hover round it, murmuring,
    Like bees at honey-time.

Upon a little Girl I look,
    Whose pureness makes me sad ;
I read as in a blessed book—
    I grow in secret glad !
It seems my darling comes to me
    With something I have lost,
Over Life's tossed and troubled sea,
    On some celestial coast.

That grave content, and touching grace,
    Bring tears into mine eyes ;
She makes my heart a holy place,
    Where hymns and incense rise.

Such calm her gentle spirit brings,
   As—smiling overhead—
White statued saints with peaceful wings,
   Shadow the sleeping dead.

Meek as the wood anemone glints,
   To see if Heaven be blue,
Is my pale flower with her sweet tints
   Of heaven shining thro'?
She will be poor, and never fret;
   Sleep sound and lowly lie;
Will live her quiet life and let
   The great world-storm go by.

Our Christie is no Rosy Grace,
   With beauty all may see;
But I have never felt a face
   Grow half so dear to me!
No curling hair about her brows,
   Like many merry Girls;
Well; straighter to my heart it goes;
   And round it curls, and curls.

I think of Her when spirit-bowed;
   A glory fills the place;
Like sudden light on swords the proud
   Smile flashes in my face!

And others see in passing by,
　　But cannot understand,
The vision shining in mine eye ;
　　My strength of heart and hand.

Dear love ! God keep her in his grasp ;
　　Meek Maiden or brave Wife ;
Till His good angels softly clasp
　　Her closèd book of Life :
And this fair picture of the Sun,
　　With Birthday blessings given,
Shall fade before a glorious one
　　Taken of her in heaven.

THE NEST.

I BUILT my Nest by a pleasant stream,
That glided on with a smile in its gleam,
 Bringing me gold that was sumless;
Ah, me! but the floods came drowning one day,
And swept my Nest with its wealth away;
 I in the world was homeless!

I built my Nest in a gay green tree,
And the summer of life went merrily
 With us! we were Birds of a feather!
But the leaves soon fell, and my pretty ones flew,
And thro' my Nest the bitter winds blew;
 'Twas bare in the wildest weather.

I built my Nest under Heaven's high eaves;
No rising of floods, no falling of leaves,
 Can mock my heart's endeavour;
Waters may wash, breezes may blow,
In the bosom of Rest I shall smile, I shall know
 My Nest is safe for ever.

OUR

LITTLE CHILD WITH RADIANT EYES.

WITH seeking hearts we still grope on,
  Where dropt our jewel in the dust;
The looking crowd have long since gone,
  And still we seek with lonely trust;
  O little Child with radiant eyes!

Dark underneath the brightening sod,
  The sweetest life of all our years
Is crowded in ae gift to God.
  We stand outside the gate in tears!
  O little Child with radiant eyes!

In all our heart-ache we are drawn,
  Unweeting, to your little grave;
There, on your heavenly shore of dawn,
  Breaks gentlier Sorrow's sobbing wave;
  O little Child with radiant eyes!

Heart-empty as the acorn-cup
  That only fills with wintry showers,
The breaking cloud but brimmeth up
  With tears this pleading life of ours.
  O little Child with radiant eyes!

We think of you, our Angel kith,
   Till life grows light with starry leaven :
We never forget you Darling with
   The gold hair waving high in heaven !
   Our little Child with radiant eyes !

Your white wings grown you will conquer Death !
   You are coming through our dreams even now,
With two blue peeps of heaven beneath
   The arching glory of your brow,
   Our little Child with radiant eyes !

We cannot pierce the dark, but oft
   You see us with looks of pitying balm ;
A hint of heaven—a touch more soft
   Than kisses—all the trouble is calm.
   O little Child with radiant eyes !

Think of us wearied in the strife ;
   And when we sit by Sorrow's streams,
Shake down upon our drooping life
   The dew that brings immortal dreams.
   O little Child with radiant eyes !

ROBIN'S SONG.

Sing, Robin Redbreast,
   Tho' you fill our hearts with pain;
Sing, bonny Robin,
   Tho' our tears fall like the rain
For a Lamb far from the fold,
In the wet and wintry mould!
For a Bird out in the cold,
     Bird alane! Bird alane!

Sing, Robin Redbreast!
   You are welcome to our door;
Sing, darling Robin,
   Merry Larks no longer soar.
Autumn comes with feel of rain,
Mournful odours, wail of pain!
There's a Bird will come again
     Nevermore! Nevermore!

Sing, Robin Redbreast!
   For we love your song so brave,
Tho' you mind us of a Robin
   Where the willows weep and wave;

To *her* little grave it clings,
Shakes the rain from its wet wings,
And for all the sadness sings
    By Her grave, by Her grave.

THE TWO ROSES.

SOFTLY stept she over the lawn,
  In vesture light and free :
A floating Angel might have drawn
Her hair from heaven in a glory-dawn,
  And her voice rang silverly.
Then up she rose on her tiny tip-toes ;
Her white hand catches, her fingers close ;
You are tall and proud my dainty Rose !
  But I have you now, said She.

O so lightly over the lawn,
  Step for step went He !
Thinking how, from his hiding-place,
The war of Roses in her face,
  Dear Love would laugh to see !
Two arms suddenly round her he throws ;
Two mouths turning one way close ;
You are tall and proud my dainty Rose !
  But I have you now, said He.

POOR MARGARET.

Poor Margaret's window is alight ;
    Poor Margaret sits alone ;
Though long into the silent night,
    And far, the world is gone.
She lives in shadow till her blood
    Grows bitter and blackened all ;
Upon her head a mourning hood ;
    Upon her heart a pall.

The stars come nightly out of heaven,
    Old darkness to beguile ;
For her there is no healing given
    To their sweet spirit-smile.
That honey-dew of sleep the skies
    In blessed balm let fall,
Comes not to her poor tired eyes,
    Tho' it be sent for all.

At some dead flower, with fragrance faint,
  Her life opes like a book ;
Some old sweet music makes its plaint,
  And, from the grave's dim nook,
The buried bud of hopes laid low,
  Flowers in the night full-blown ;
And little things of Long-Ago
  Come back to her full-grown.

Her heart is wandering in a whirl,
  And she must seek the tomb
Where lies her long-lost little girl.
  O well with them for whom
Love's Morning-Star comes round so fair
  As Evening-Star of Faith,
Already up and shining, ere
  The dark of coming death.

But, Margaret cannot reach a hand,
  Beyond the dark of death ;
Her spirit swoons in that high land
  Where breathes no human breath ;
She cannot look upon the grave
  As one eternal shore ;
From which a soul may take the wave,
  For heaven, to sail or soar.

Across that Deep no sail unfurled,
    For her ; no wings put forth ;
She tries to reach the other world
    By groping down through earth.
'T was there the child went underground ;
    They parted in that place ;
And ever since, the Mother found
    The door shut in her face.

Tho' many effacing springs have wrapped
    With green, the dark grave-bed ;
'Twas *there*, the breaking heartstrings snapped
    As she let down her dead :
And there she gropes with wild heart yet,
    For years, and years, and years ;
Poor Margaret ! there she will let
    Her sorrows loose in tears.

All the young mother in her old voice
    Its waking moan will make !
A young aurora light her eyes
    With radiance gone to wreck !
And then at dawn she will return,
    To her old self again ;
Eyes dim and dry ; heart grey and dern ;
    And querulous in her pain.

" We never loved each other much,
   I and my poor good-man ;
But on the Child we lavisht such
   A love as overran
All boundaries, loving her the more
   Because our love was pent ;
Striving as two seas try to pour
   Their strength thro' one small rent.

" For children come to still link hands,
   When souls have fallen apart ;
And hide the rift, when either stands
   At distance heart from heart.
So on our little one we 'd look ;
   Press hands with fonder grasp ;
As tho' we closed some holy book,
   Softly, with golden clasp.

" And as the dark earth offers up
   Her little winterling,
The Crocus, pleading with its cup
   Of hoarded gold, to bring
Down all the grey heaven's golden shower
   Of spring to warm the sod ;
So did we lift the winsome flower
   That sprang from our dark clod.

"Our little Golden-heart, her name !
 And all things sweet and calm,
And pure and fragrant round her came
 With gifts of bloom and balm.
And there she grew, my queen of all,
 Golden, and saintly white ;
Just as at Summer's smiling call
 The lily stands a-light.

"To knee or nipple, grew the goal
 Of her wee stately walk ;
The voice of my own silent soul
 Was her dear baby-talk ;
Then darklingly she pined and failed ;
 And looking on our dead,
The father wailed awhile and ailed,
 Turned to the wall and said—

"'Tis dark and still, our house of life,
 The fire is burning low ;
Our pretty one is gone, and Wife,
 'Tis time for me to go :
Our Golden-heart has gone to sleep ;
 She's happed in for the night ;
And so to bed I'll quietly creep,
 And sleep till morning light.'"

Once more poor Margaret arose,
    And passed into the night:
Long shadows weird of tree and house
    Made ghosts i' the wan moonlight!
She passed into the churchyard, where
    The many glad life-waves
That leapt of old, have stood still there,
    In green and grassy graves.

"O would my body were at rest
    Under this cool grave-sward:
O would my soul were with the Blest,
    That slumber in the Lord!
They sleep so sweetly underground;
    For Death hath shut the door,
And all the world of sorrow and sound
    Can trouble them no more."

A spirit-feel is in the place,
    That makes the poor heart gasp;
Her soul stands white up in her face
    For one warm human clasp!
Tonight she sees the grave astir;
    And as in prayer she kneels,
The mystery opens unto her:
    She for the first time feels

The spirit-world may be as near
　　Her moving silent round,
As are the dead that sleep a mere
　　Short fathom underground;
And there be eyes that see the sight
　　Of lorn ones wandering, vexed
Thro' some long, sad, and shadowy night
　　Betwixt this world and next.

Doorways of fear, are eye and ear,
　　Thro' which the wonders go;
And thro' the night with glow-worm light,
　　The Church is all aglow!
Then comes a waft of Sabbath hymn;
　　She enters; all the air
With faces fills divine and dim,
　　The Blessed Dead are there.

One came and bade poor Margaret sit,
　　Seemed to her as it smiled,
A great white Bird of God alit
　　From the marble forest wild.
" Look to the Altar!" there a spell
　　Fixed her; she saw up-start,
A woman, like a soul in hell,
　　'T was her own Golden-heart.

" It would have been thus, Mother dear,
   And so God took her, from
All trials and temptations here,
   To his eternal home ;
And you shall see her in a place
   Where death can never part."
She lookt up in that Angel's face ;
   'T was her own Golden-heart.

The lofty music rose again
   From all those happy souls,
Till all the windows thrilled, as when
   The organ thunder rolls ;
And all her life is like a light
   Weak weed the stream doth sway,
Until it reaches the full-height ;
   Breaks, and is borne away.

Her life stood still to listen to
   That music ! then a hand
Took hers, and she was floated through
   A mystic border-land.
'T was Golden-heart ! from that eclipse
   She drew her into bliss ;
Two spirits closed at dying lips,
   In one immortal kiss.

Next day an early worshipper
   Was kneeling in the Aisle;
A statue of life that did not stir,
   But knelt on with a smile
Upon the face that smiled with light,
   As tho', when left behind,
It smiled on with some glorious sight
   Long after the eyes were blind.

LULLABY.

Softly sink in slumbers golden,
  Warm as nestled Birdlings lie ;
Safe in Mother's arms enfolden,
  While I sing thy lullaby.
Lullaby, lullaby, lullaby, lullaby,
Sweet one, sleep to my Lullaby.

Tho' the night may darken, darken,
  Light will Mother's slumbers lie ;
Still my heart will hearken, hearken,
  Lest my wee thing wake and cry.
Lullaby, lullaby, lullaby, lullaby,
Sweet one, sleep to my Lullaby.

At thy garden gate of slumber,
  Stands my spirit tiptoe high,
Filled with yearnings without number,
  In thine inner heaven to fly.
Lullaby, lullaby, lullaby, lullaby,
Sweet one, sleep to my Lullaby.

In that world of mystic breathing,
   Spirit Sentinels, stand by !
Winnow, winnow, o'er my wee thing,
   Wings of Love that hover nigh.
Lullaby, lullaby, lullaby, lullaby,
Sweet one, sleep to my Lullaby.

Sleep ! and drink the dew delicious !
   Sleep ! till the morrow dawn is high !
Sleep with Mother near her precious,
   Wake ! with Mother waiting nigh.
Lullaby, lullaby, lullaby, lullaby,
Sweet one, sleep to my Lullaby.

HOW THE FLOWERS CAME FROM EDEN.

THE Seraph faded into air;
   The Snake glode underground;
As on the last step of Heaven's stair,
   Poor exiled Eve lookt round.

Heartless as Death, and blind as Doom,
   The heavens bowed with wrath :
Where God, betwixt the glare and gloom,
   Stood in their backward path.

The memories in each other's eyes,
   They cannot, dare not face ;
Forlorn and vast the wide world lies ;
   They see no hiding place.

Two mourners following the hearse
   Of joy, go slowly forth ;
To see the shadow of their curse
   Fall lengthening over earth.

Then did the Flowers of Eden grieve ;
　　As tho' a low wind stirred,
They softly prayed to follow Eve ;
　　And God in Heaven heard.

As when some erring Child may see,
　　The Father's face no more ;
A Mother's love sends secretly ;
　　Her heart keeps open door ;

So were the Flowers from Paradise,
　　For missioned comfort sent ;
All heaven in their sweet pitying eyes !
　　And where Eve trod they went.

With dear drops of that gladness spilled
　　In Eden, they came pearled ;
Their cups with colours of Heaven filled,
　　To pour thro' all the world.

They kiss her feet ; embrace her knees ;
　　About her dance and play ;
They run before and climb the trees,
　　To cheer her by the way.

On hills and moorlands golden fires
   Of gorse in beauty burn ;
Into red roses break the briars ;
   A flower for every thorn.

And ever since, their silent march,
   Goes glowing overground ;
And under Ocean's azure arch ;
   In an immortal round.

The wee white fairies of the snow,
   May cover them awhile ;
But from their hiding-places, lo !
   The fresh young Eden smile !

They come back with their fragrant news,
   By brook, and field, and fell ;
They wake, and in a thousand hues,
   Their dream of beauty tell.

They bring the distant dearness of
   That dewy Eden youth,
Into the kindling nearness of
   Warm kisses on the mouth.

Our thoughts are with their fancies freakt,
　　And delicately drawn ;
With them our gray of life is streakt,
　　Divinely as the dawn.

And ailing souls come forth to see,
　　How the sweet Flowers reveal
The waving skirts of Deity,
　　Which at a touch can heal.

Our dying eyes their balm beseech ;
　　Our dying fingers fold
Their coolness, when we cannot reach
　　The flower ; so dank the mould.

Their roots like feeling fingers twine,
　　About the lone grave-bed :
Stars of the ground, they kindly shine,
　　Thro' that long dark o' the Dead.

Incense, pathetically sweet,
　　Their little censers wave—
Standing all night at head and feet
　　Of our wee Sydney's grave.

With mournful fragrance to my heart,
   They pierce at times, until
The tears up in mine eyes will start,
   With airs of heaven a-thrill.

Still blooms with all its buried charms,
   That old lost land of ours ;
Above its silent war of worms,
   A world laughs out in flowers.

ONE WHO WAS KIND TO CHRISTIE.

God comfort you, my friend, God comfort you!
How mighty, how immeasurable your loss
I can but dimly know; yet I have learned
That only the most precious die so soon.
I can but stand without, and dare not thrust
My hand betwixt the curtains of your grief;
I cannot reach you sitting in the dark
Of that lone desert where the silence stuns,
And sound of sobbing would be kind relief.
But might I speak some word that, with a touch,
Should make your cup of sorrow overbrim
In tears that suck the sting from out the soul!
I too have felt the gloom that brings heaven near,
The love whose kissings are all unreturned,
And longed to lie down with the quiet dead
And share their long sweet rest. I too have known
This strain and crack of heart-strings—this wild whirl
And wallow of sense in which the soul seems drowned.

You are the husband of an angel: I
Have two sweet Babes in bliss. We are very poor
On earth, my Friend, but very rich in Heaven.

Two years ago you comforted my loss:
One year ago I sang your wedding song,
And now She is not! She who had only lookt
On life thro' coloured windows of her dreams!
All in the softest, sweetest breath of God
The bud of her dear beauty seemed to have blown,
Your one-year darling who but sprang, and died,
And left the fragrance of her memory;
A blessed memory and a blessed hope!
She had the shy grace of a woodland flower;
In her Love veiled his look with timid wings;
And her eyes deepened with a sadness rich,
As tho' the mountain-tops of heaven-toucht thought
Made mirrored shadows in their lakes of light.
Only a brief while did she wear the mask
Of flesh that kept the fond immortal face
Without a stain of earth or soil of time;
And now her Nun-like spirit takes the veil
In Heaven's cloistral calm.

           Look up, my friend,
And bravely bear the mantle of her pain,
Which fell from her for you to wear for her!

Look up, my friend, and may one blessed glimpse
Of all her glory touch your tears with light!
Only in heaven can the dark grow starry,
Only in heaven comes the wished-for dawn.
She liveth in the sight of Him that sees
You also; Ye are one still in God's eye
That from his picture of the Universe
Turns on us in whatever worlds we move.

THE MAIDEN MARRIAGE.

SHE sat in her virgin bower
  Half sad with fancies sweet ;
And wist not Love drew softly nigh,
  Till she nestled at his feet.
" Arise, arise, thou fair Maiden !
  And adieu, adieu, thou dear ;
But meet me, meet me at the Kirk,
  In the May-time of the year."

Up in her face of holy grace
  The startled splendour broke ;
Her smile was as a dream of Heaven
  Fulfilled whene'er she spoke.
She felt such bliss in her beauty,
  Such pleasure in her power,
To richly clothe her perfect love
  For a peerless marriage dower.

Q

"Now kiss me, kiss me, Mother dear;
　　He calls me, I must go!"
She went to the Kirk at tryste-time,
　　In raiment like the snow.
But he who claspt her there was Death;
　　And he hath led her where
No voice is heard, there is no breath
　　Upon the frosty air.

A POET.

A VAGRANT Wild Flower sown by God,
   Out in the waste was born;
It sprang up as a Corn-flower
   In the golden fields of Corn:
The Corn all strong and stately
   In its bearded bravery grew—
Gathered the gold for harvest—
   Grew ripe, in sun and dew;
And when it bowed the head,—as Wind
   And Shadów ran their race,
As influences from Heaven
   Come to Earth, for playing place,—
It seemed to look down on the Flower
   As in a smiling scorn,
Poor thing! you grow no grain for food,
   Or garner, said the Corn.

The bonny Flower felt lonely;
  Its look grew tearful sad,
Till came a smile of sunshine
  And its beauty grew so glad!
Ah, bonny Flower! it bloomed its best
  Contented with its place;
God's blessing fell upon it
  As it lookt up in his face.
And there they grew together
  Till the Reapers white-wing'd came—
All their Sickles shining!
  All their faces were a-flame;—
The Corn they reapt for earthly use,—
  But an Immortal fell in love
With that Wild Flower, and wore it
  At the Harvest-home above.

LIFE AND DEATH.

This butterfly of human breath,
Is followed fast and far by Death;
Some flower of life it settled on
He clasps and crushes; but, 't is gone!

POOR BIDDY.

Poor Biddy was peculiarly proud,
And often passed along the public road
Riding a Stick: she would have been a witch
In the old days, and wierdly filled her niche.

The mocking Bairns would cry, as she would stalk,
" Biddy, you might as well on two legs walk ;"
And she would say, says she, the poor daftling !
" I might ! but for the grandeur of the thing."

Alas, how many pitiful tricks we play
Like Biddy, in less Natural kind o' way :
And ride our stick, and have our foolish fling,
God help us ! for the grandeur of the thing.

WHEN CHRISTIE COMES AGAIN.

WHEN the merry spring-tide
   Floods all the land,
Nature hath a Mother's heart—
   Gives with open hand.
Flowers running up the lane
   Tell us May is near;
Christie will be coming then,
   Christie will be here.
O, the merry spring-tide,
   We'll be glad in sun or rain,
In the merry, merry, merry days
   When Christie comes again.

Pure is her meek nature,
   Clear as morning dew;
We can see the Angel
   Almost shining through.
To Earth's sweetest blessing
   She the best from Heaven did bring;

Good Genius of our Love-Lamp!
  Fine Spirit of the Ring!
O, the merry spring-tide,
  We'll be glad in sun or rain,
In the merry, merry, merry days
  When Christie comes again.

All our joys we'll tell her,
  But for her dear sake
Not a word of sorrow,
  Lest her little heart should ache.
She shall dance, and swing, and sing,
  Do as she likes best;
Only I must have her hand
  In ramble or in rest.
O, the merry spring-tide,
  We'll be glad in sun or rain,
In the merry, merry, merry days
  When Christie comes again.

We'll romp in jewelled meadows,
  Hunt in dingles, cool with leaves,
Where all night the Nightingale
  Melodiously grieves.
In her cheek so tender,
  The shy and dainty rose

Shall gaily come for kisses
    To every wind that blows :
O, the merry spring-tide,
    We'll be glad in sun or rain,
In the merry, merry, merry days
    When Christie comes again.

Hope will lay so many eggs
    In her little nest :
Don't your heart run over,
    Christie, in your breast ?
Ours will run to meet you,
    Often ere you come ;
Thinking how we'll greet you,
    Safe once more at home.
O, the merry spring-tide,
    We'll be glad in sun or rain,
In the merry, merry, merry days
    When Christie comes again.

Oh, the joy in our house,
    Hearts dancing wild ;
Christie will be coming soon,
    She's our darling child.
Holy dew of Heaven,
    In each eyelid starts,

Feeling all her dearness,
    Darling of all hearts.
O, the merry spring-tide,
    We'll be glad in sun or rain,
In the merry, merry, merry days
    When Christie comes again.

Dreary was our winter,
    Come ! and all the place
Shall breathe a summer sweetness,
    And wear a happy face.
There will be a sun-smile
    On stern old Calliby,
Tender as the spring-gold
    On our old oak-tree !
O, the merry spring-tide,
    We'll be glad in sun or rain,
In the merry, merry, merry days
    When Christie comes again.

Jack, the Dog, will run before,
    First to reach the rail ;
Jack, the Pony, whisk you home
    With long trotting tail ;
We have had our struggles, Dear !
    But couldn't part with Jack,

We shall all be waiting
　　To welcome Christie back.
O, the merry spring-tide,
　　We'll be glad in sun or rain,
In the merry, merry, merry days
　　When Christie comes again.

Then blow, you winds, and shake up
　　The sleeping flower-beds !
Make the violets wake up,
　　The Daisies lift their heads ;
The Lilacs float in fragrance,
　　Dim-purple, saintly white,—
And bring the bonny bairn to us,
　　The flower of our delight.
O, the merry spring-tide,
　　We'll be glad in sun or rain,
In the merry, merry, merry days
　　When Christie comes again.

DOWN IN THE VILLAGE.

A LETTER IN BLACK.

A FLOATING on the fragrant flood
　　Of summer,—fuller hour by hour,—
With all the sweetness of the bud
　　Crowned by the glory of the flower;
My spirits with the season flowed;
　　The air was all a breathing balm;
The lake so softly sapphire glowed;
　　The mountains lay in royal calm.

Green leaves were lusty; roses blusht
　　For pleasure in the golden time;
The birds thro' all their feathers flusht
　　For gladness of their marriage prime:
Languid, among the lilies I threw
　　Me down, for coolness, 'mid the sheen:
Heaven—one large smile of brooding blue;
　　Earth—one large smile of basking green.

A rich suspended shower of gold
   Hung o'er me, my Laburnum-crown,
You look up heavenward and, behold,
   It glows, and comes in glory down!
There, as my thoughts of greenness grew
   To fruitage of a leafy dream,—
There, friend, your letter thrilled me through,
   And all the summer-day was dim.

The world, so pleasant to the sight,
   So full of voices blithe and brave,
And all her lamps of beauty alight
   With life!   I had forgot the Grave:
And there it opened at my feet,
   Revealing a familiar face
Upturned, my whitened look to meet,
   And very patient in its place.

My poor bereaven friend! I know
   Not how to word it, but would bring
A little solace for your woe,—
   A little love for comforting:
And yet the best that I can say
   Will only help to sum your loss;
I can but look above, and pray
   God help my friend to bear his Cross.

I have felt something of your smart,
    And lost the dearest thing e'er wound
In love about a human heart:
    I, too, have life-roots underground.
From out my soul hath leapt a cry
    For help! Nor God himself could save:
And tears still run that nought will dry,
    Save Death's hand with the dust o' the grave.

God knows, and we may some day know,
    These hidden secrets of his love;
But now the stillness stuns us so;
    Darkly, as in a dream, we move.
The glad life-pulses come and go,
    Over our head and at our feet;
Soft airs are sighing something low;
    The flowers are saying something sweet:

And 'tis a merry world. The lark
    Is singing over the green corn;
Only the house and heart are dark,—
    Only the human world forlorn.
There, in the bridal chamber, lies
    A dear bed-fellow all in white;
That purple shadow under the eyes,
    Where star-fire swam in liquid night.

Sweet, slippery silver of her talk ;
 The music of her laugh so dear,
Heard in home-ways, and wedded walk,
 For many and many a golden year ;
The singing soul and shining face,
 Daisy-like glad by roughest road ;
Gone ! with a thousand dearnesses
 That hid themselves for us and glowed.

The waiting Angel, patient Wife,
 All thro' the battle at our side,
That smiled her sweetness on our strife
 For gain, and it was sanctified !
When waves of trouble beat breast high
 And the heart sank, she poured a balm
That stilled them ; and the saddest sky
 Made clear and starry with her calm.

And when the world with harvest ripe
 In all its golden fulness lay ;
And God, it seemed, saw fit to wipe,
 Even on earth, all tears away ;
The good true heart that bravely won,
 Must smile up in our face and fall ;
And all our happy days are done,
 And this the end.   And is this all ?

The bloom of bliss, the secret glow,
 That clothed without, and inly curled,
All gone, we are left shivering now,
 Naked to the wide open world!
A shrivelled, withered, world it is,
 And sad and miserably cold;
Where be its vaunted braveries?
 'Tis gray, and miserably old.

Our joy was all a drunken dream;
 This is the truth at waking! we
Are swept out rootless by the stream
 And current of calamity—
Out on some lone and shoreless sea
 Of solitude so vast and deep,
As 'twere a wrong Eternity,
 Where God is not, or gone to sleep.

It seems as tho' our darling dead,
 Startled at Death's so sudden call,
With falling hands and dear bowed head
 Had, like a flower-filled lap, let fall
A hoard of treasures we have found
 Too late! so slow doth wisdom come!
We for the first time look around
 Remembering this is not our home.

My friend, I see you with your cup
　　Of tears and trembling—see you sit ;
And long to help you drink it up,
　　With useless longings infinite !—
Sit rocking the old mournful thought,
　　That on the heart's-blood will be nurst,
Unless the blessed tears be brought ;
　　Unless the cloudy sorrows burst.

The little ones are gone to rest,
　　And for awhile they will not miss
The Mother-wings above the nest :
　　But down a dream they feel her kiss,
And in their sleep will sometimes start,
　　And toss wild arms for her caress,
With moanings that must thrill a heart
　　In heaven with divine distress.

And Sorrow on your threshold stands,
　　The Dark Ladye in glooming pall :
I see her take you by the hands ;
　　I feel her shadow over all.
Her's is no warm and tender clasp ;
　　With silence solemn as the night's,
And veilèd face, and mighty grasp,
　　She leads her Chosen up the heights :

The cloudy crags are cold and gray,
　　You cannot scale them without scars :
So many Martyrs by the way,
　　Who never reacht her tower of stars,
But there her beauty shall be seen,
　　Her glittering face so proudly pure ;
And all her majesty of mien ;
　　And all her guerdon shall be sure.

Well.　'Tis not written, God will give
　　To his Beloved only rest !
The hard life of the cross they live,
　　They strive, and suffer, and are blest.
The feet must bleed to reach their throne,
　　The brow must burn before it bear
One of the crowns that may be won,
　　By workers for immortal wear.

Dear friend, life beats tho' buried 'neath
　　Its long black vault of night ! and see
There trembles thro' this dark of death,
　　Starlight of immortality !
And yet shall dawn the eternal day
　　To kiss the eyes of them that sleep ;
And He shall wipe all tears away
　　From tired eyes of them that weep.

'Tis something for the poor bereaven,
   In such a weary world of care,
To think that we have friends in heaven;
   Who helpt us here, may aid us there.
These yearnings for them set our arc
   Of being widening more and more,
In circling sweep thro' outer dark
   To day more perfect than before.

So much was left unsaid, the soul
   Must live in other worlds to be;
On earth we cannot grasp the whole,
   For that Love has eternity.
Love deep as death, and rich as rest;
   Love that was love with all Love's might;
Level to needs the lowliest;
   Will not be less Love at full-height.

Tho' earthly forms be far apart,
   Spirit to spirit may be nigher;
The music chord the same at heart,
   Tho' one should range an octave higher.
Eyes watch us that we cannot see;
   Lips warn us which we may not kiss;
They wait for us, and starrily,
   Lean toward us from heaven's lattices.

We cannot see them face to face,
   But love is nearness ; and they love
Us yet, nor change, with change of place,
   In their more human world above,
Where love, once leal, hath never ceased,
   And dear eyes never lose their shine,
And there shall be a marriage feast,
   Where Christ shall once more make the wine.

FARMER FORREST'S OPINION OF THE
BROAD-BOTTOMED MINISTRY.

1859.

Now tell me you who wink, or blink, or think,
What good is a *Broad* bottom if we sink?

Not Whigs! not Tories! we want English souls
Where-thro' there yet reverberates and rolls
Some echo of old greatness; good stout hands
Must bear our Banner over seas and lands!
Our forms of freedom must not choke the breath,
The outer mail be forged for inner death!
There is a wild hour coming for us, when
We must all weather it as Englishmen.

We cannot leave the land for watch and ward
To those who know not what a gem they guard;
Who bind us helpless for the Bird of Blood
To swoop on; who would have this famous flood
Of English Freedom stagnate till it stink,
While reptiles wriggle in their slimy drink,
And frogs shall reign in darkness; croak all night
And call the Stars false Prophets of the light.

Our good ship may be driving on the rocks:
We want a Compass, and not Weather-Cocks!
We have had leaders who strode forward all
On fire to serve her at their Country's call;
They did not stoop, till blind, for place and pelf,
Their whole life burned a sacrifice of self!
They faced the Spirit of the Storm and Strife,
And with an upward smile laid down their life.

But now our leaders are the coward and cold;
The Gnomes whose daylight is a gleam of gold;
The Dwarfs who sun them in a Tyrant's smile;
The Peacemen who would set our dear green Isle
Spinning their Cotton till the judgment hour,
With Ocean turning round for water-power.
These pander to this Plunderer of the night;
Confused their little sense of Wrong and Right!
And they would bow our England's dear head down
Trustfully in his lap to leave her crown!
See her sit weeping where her brave lie dead;
Blood on her raiment, ashes on her head.

A Palmerston now crawls were Cromwell stood;
A Tyrant's Parasite, that licks the blood
From his red hand, an old eternal stain!
And takes, for Glory's sign, that brand of Cain!

He is an Eve in innocence we know,
But leans and listens to the Serpent so,
We are no safer although well we weet
The fruit of knowledge He will never eat.

In Milton's patriot seat sits little John,
Who to the muzzle loads his monster gun,
And fires in air if it goes off at all,
To find his own lead on his own head fall,
If he have any, for, since he who bled
Upon a Tyrant's block *once* lost his head,
To keep up the tradition Lord John is
Determined to be *always* losing his.

And Gladstone aims at nothing, sure to hit,
Or splits fine hairs till he have none to split.
Who rides out from the ranks for challenge, he
May toss the Sword and catch it gracefully,
But *must* be able, when the onsets come,
To drive with slaying hand his hilt heart-home.
He is a Seer, but so many-eyed,
He sees so many ways, from many a side,
His eyes like horses in the old punishment
Whereby all ways at once the doomed was rent,
Draw to divide him, follow if he dare,
He is to pieces pulled by either pair.

These be our Leaders now.   Napoleon's Pal,
Is head of England's power, and crowning all,
To cool the blood, and soothe all sin to rest,
The great castrated Quaker Interest
Stands Eunuch at the Privy Chamber.
                                        Wake
My England! *these* thy sword and shield? they make
A Ministry broad-bottomed without doubt,
For better target when you kick them out.

MY BONNY LADY.

Eve gave us her fair Daughters to restore
The Eden that their Mother lost of yore;
They lead us thro' the Angel-guarded door,
And where they smile it blooms for evermore.
But dearest of Eve's Daughters dear is she
Who makes an Eden in my Home for me;

My Bonny Lady.

No seeming beauty perilous to know,
Like dream of ripeness on the sour sloe,
But sweet to the true heart as summer fruit,
And sound and strong to love's most secret root;
A soul made human by its kindling life!
A woman ripened to the perfect Wife!

My Bonny Lady.

She grows in graces as the flowers bloom;
Her robe of beauty woven in Heaven's loom!
She wears her jewels in her lips and eyes:
Diamond sparks! warm rubies! pearls of price!
And see what shapely sweetness may be shown,
Bright budding from a simple morning gown!

My Bonny Lady.

Upon her dear brow is no band of care
That binds the heavy burden souls must bear;
The dew of childhood's Heaven yet lingering lies
Cool in the shadows of her morning eyes;
So may some spirit in its brightness wait
With welcome at the beautiful heaven gate.

My Bonny Lady.

Eyelids once lifted with the kiss of Love,
Droop tender after as the brooding dove!
Lips, when the soul of joy is tasted, will
Hush its loud sound of laughter, and be still.
Yet is she happy as the lark that sings,
Winnowing out the music with his wings;

My Bonny Lady.

Lo, how she bows with soft and settled bliss,
Over her babe in breathless tenderness !
Her image that my Lily bends above,
To mingle One in my heart's sea of Love !
Thus hath she doubled love and Love's caress,
With doubled blessing, doubled power to bless.

My Bonny Lady.

Her smile the sum of sweetness infinite !
Her neck a throne where many graces sit !
Like music of the soul her motion is,
But none can know the inner sanctities ;
Outside they stand in wonder, I alone
Pass in to worship at the spirit-throne.

My Bonny Lady.

Behold her in religious lustre stand,
Clothed all in white and fit for spirit-land !
Her thankful eyes uplift for angel food ;
And you might worship her, so pure, so good ;
For all shy beauty, all sweet shadowy grace,
Breaks into brightness through my Lady's face ;

My Bonny Lady.

I think of her, and mine eyes softly close
While all my heart with sweetness overflows;
Each breath it breathes in blessing sets astir
Some gracious balm, and sweet as hidden myrrh.
My Rest while toiling up the hill of life!
A Halfway House to Heaven! my noble Wife!

My Bonny Lady.

ON A WEDDING DAY.

Thus, hand in hand, and heart in heart,
 Face nestling unto face,
Forgotten things like Spirits start
 From many a hiding place !
There is no sound of Babe or Bird,
 And all the stillness seems
Sweet as the music only heard
 Adown the land of dreams.

And if, because it is so proud,
 My heart will find a voice,
And in its dear dream love aloud,
 And speak of sweet still joys,
It is no genuine gift of God,
 But only goblin gold,
That withers into dead leaves, should
 The secret tale be told.

Nine years ago you came to me,
  And nestled on my breast,
A soft and wingèd mystery
  That settled here to rest ;
And my heart rockt its Babe of bliss,
  And soothed its child of air,
With something 'twixt a song and kiss,
  To keep it nestling there.

At first I thought the fairy form
  Too spirit-soft and good
To fill my poor, low nest with warm
  And wifely womanhood.
But such a cozy peep of home
  Did your dear eyes unfold ;
And in their deep and dewy gloom
  What tales of love were told !

In dreamy curves your beauty droopt,
  As tendrils lean to twine,
And very graciously they stoopt
  To bear their fruit, my Vine !
To bear such blessed fruit of love
  As tenderly increased
Among the ripe vine-bunches of
  Your balmy-breathing breast.

We cannot boast to have bickered not
    Since you and I were wed ;
We have not lived the smoothest lot,
    Nor found the downiest bed !
Time hath not passed o'er-head in stars,
    And underfoot in flowers,
With wings that slept on fragrant airs
    Thro' all the happy hours.

It is our way, more fate than fault,
    Love's cloudy fire to clear ;
To find some virtue in the salt
    That sparkles in a tear !
Pray God it all come right at last,
    Pray God it so befall,
That when our day of life is past
    The end may crown it all.

Ah, Dear ! tho' lives may pull apart
    Down to the roots of love,
One thought will bend us heart to heart,
    Till lips re-wed above !
One thought the knees of pride will bow
    Down to the grave-yard sod ;
You are the Mother of Angels now !
    We have two babes with God.

Cling closer, closer, for their loss,
    About our darlings left,
And let their memories grow like moss
    That healeth rent and rift;—
For his dear sake, our Soldier Boy,
    For whom we nightly plead
That he may live for God, and die
    For England in her need:

For her, who like a dancing boat
    Leaps o'er life's solemn waves,
Our little Lightheart who can float
    And frolic over graves;
And Grace, who making music goes,
    As in some shady place
A brooklet, prattling to the boughs,
    Looks up with its bright face.

Cling closer, closer, life to life,
    Cling closer, heart to heart;
The time will come, my own wed Wife,
    When you and I must part!
Let nothing break our band but Death,
    For in the worlds above
'Tis the breaker Death that soldereth
    Our ring of Wedded Love.

MARRIAGE.

Two human Stars in passing are
   Attracted as thro' Heaven they float ;
Sometimes they form a double Star,
   Sometimes they put each other out :
And sometimes one and one make three,
This world's most perfect trinity.

UNDER THE MISLETOE.

'T was on a merry Christmas night,
　　A many years ago,
I saw my Love, with dancing sight,
　　As she came over the snow.
The Elvish Holly laught above;
　　A sweeter red below!
When first I met with my true love,
　　Under the Misletoe Bough.

Bright-headed as the merry May Dawn
　　She floated down the dance:
I thought some angel must have gone
　　Our human way by chance.
I held my hands, and caught my bliss.
　　Children, I 'll show you how!
And Earth toucht Heaven in a kiss,
　　Under the Misletoe Bough.

Ere leaves were green we built our nest,
　　The March winds whistled wild ;
But in our love we were so blest
　　Old Poverty he smiled.
And Love the heart of Winter warmed ;
　　Love blossomed 'neath the snow ;
All fairyland in blessings swarmed,
　　Under the Misletoe Bough.

The storms of years have beat our Bark,
　　That rocks at anchor now ;
But She was smiling thro' the dark,
　　My Angel at the prow.
And brimming tides of love did bear
　　Us over the rocks below !
To-night, all safe in harbour here,
　　Under the Misletoe Bough.

May you, Boys, win just such a Wife ;
　　Come drink the toast in wine !
And you, Girls, may you light a life
　　As she hath brightened mine.
Dear was the bonny Bride, and yet
　　I 'm prouder of her now
Than on the merry, merry night we met,
　　Under the Misletoe Bough.

A VILLAGE COURTING.

O shy and simple Village Girl,
  With daisy-drooping eyes;
Like light asleep within the pearl,
  Love in your young life lies.
A hundred times in meadow and lane
  With careless hearts we walkt;
But we shall never meet again,
  And talk as we have talkt.
All in a moment life was crost,
  In a fairy spell I'm bound;
Yet fear to tell you what I've lost,
  Or know what I have found.

When last I met you, tearful-meek
  The emerald gloaming came;
Some veil fell from you, in your cheek
  The live rose was aflame!
So distant and so dear you grew,
  More near, yet more estranged,

And at your parting touch I knew
   How all the world was changed.
All in a moment life was crost,
   In a fairy spell I'm bound;
Yet fear to tell you what I've lost,
   Or know what I have found.

Your fairness haunts me all night long,
   I walk in a dream by day;
My silent heart breaks into song,
   And the prayerless kneels to pray.
Ten times a day the hot tears start,
   For very pride of you:
Would God you were safe at home in my heart,
   To rest the rough world through.
All in a moment life was crost,
   In a fairy spell I'm bound;
Yet fear to tell you what I've lost,
   Or know what I have found.

My heart! She comes by lane and stile,
   With glances shy and sweet;
Making the sunlight with her smile,
   And music with her feet.
Ah! could I clasp her in mine arm
   Until she named the hour

When life should move from charm to charm,
　And love from flower to flower!
All in a moment life was crost,
　In a fairy spell I'm bound;
Yet fear to tell her what I've lost,
　Or know what I have found.

MY LOVE.

My Love is true and tender,
  Her eyes are rich with rest;
Her hair of dappled splendour,
  The colour I love best;
So sweet, so gay, so odorous warm,
  She nestles here, heart-high;
A bounteous aspect, beauteous form,
  But—just a wee bit sly.

My love is no light Dreamer,
  A-floating with the foam;
But a brave life-sea swimmer,
  With footing found in Home.
My winsome Wife, she's bright without,
  And beautiful within;
But—I would not say quite without
  The least wee touch of sin.

My Love is not an Angel
   In one or two small things ;
But just a wifely woman
   With other wants than wings.
You have some little leaven
   Of earth, you darling dear !
If you were fit for Heaven,
   You might not nestle here.

AT EVENTIDE.

I sit beneath my shadowing Palm,
   All in the green o' the day at rest :
And pictured in a sea of calm,
   The Past arises in my breast.
The winter world takes leafy wing
   In that sweet April tide of ours ;
And hidden Love lies listening,
   And nodding smile the bridal flowers.

I sing, and shut mine eyes and dream
   I see her singing, my young Bride !
Who on a-sudden from Life's stream
   Rose Swan-like swimming at my side.
God love her ! she was very fair,
   As in her eyes, to light my way,
The Love-Star sprang and sparkled where
   The hidden Babe of Blessing lay.

With healing as of summer showers
    That only nestle down to bless :
And silent ministry of flowers,
    That only breathe their tenderness ;
She, softly as a starry scheme,
    My charmèd world hath circled round,
Till life doth seem a pleasant dream
    The victor dreameth sitting crowned.

Gone is the sunshine from her hair,
    That made her beauty needless bright,
To tint a many clouds of care,
    And make my tears to smile with light.
But so she lives that when the wind
    Of winter shreds the leaves, dear Wife !
Seed ripe for Heaven Death may find
    On the poor withered stem of life.

THE END.

T RICHARDS, 37, GREAT QUEEN STREET.